MURDER AT THE METROPOLITAN MUSEUM

MURDER AT THE METROPOLITAN MUSEUM

THE THIRD BOBBIE FLYNN MYSTERY

JACK MURRAY

Books by Jack Murray

Kit Aston Mysteries.
The Affair of the Christmas Card Killer
The Chess Board Murders.
The Phantom Museum
The Frisco Falcon
The Medium Murders
The Bluebeard Club
The Tangier Tajine
The Empire Theatre Murders
The Newmarket Murders
The New Year's Eve Murders
The French Diplomat Affair (novella)
Haymaker's Last Fight (novelette)

DI Jellicoe Mysteries
A Time to Kill
The Bus Stop
Trio
Dolce Vita Murders

Agatha Aston Mysteries
Black-Eyed Nick
The Witchfinder General Murders
The Christmas Murder Mystery
The Siegfried Slayer (Oct 2023)

Danny Shaw / Manfred Brehme WWII Series
The Shadow of War
Crusader
El Alamein

The Bobbie Flynn Mysteries
A Little Miss Taken
Murder on Tin Pan Alley
Murder at the Metropolitan

Copyright © 2024 by Jack Murray

All rights reserved. No part of this publication may be reproduced, distributed, or transmitted in any form or by any means, including photocopying, recording, or other electronic or mechanical methods, without the prior written permission of the publisher, except in the case of brief quotations embodied in critical reviews and certain other non-commercial uses permitted by copyright law. For permission requests, write to the publisher, addressed 'Attention: Permissions Coordinator,' at the address below.

Jackmurray99@hotmail.com

This is a work of fiction. Names, characters, businesses, places, events, locales, and incidents are either the products of the author's imagination or used in a fictitious manner. Any resemblance to actual persons, living or dead, or actual events is purely coincidental.

Cover by Jack Murray

ISBN: 9798326839886
Imprint: Independently published

For Monica, Lavinia, Anne, and our angel baby, Edward

1

Metropolitan Museum of Art, New York: February 1922

A tall, elegantly dressed man strode across the mosaic marble floor of the Great Hall, that welcomed thousands of visitors to the Metropolitan Museum of Art. He was a classical scholar, an archaeologist, whose association with 'the Met' went back thirty years. He was handsome and looked younger than his sixty-four years. Grey flecked his fair hair and well-groomed moustache. A few people stopped and pointed to him for, within these walls and probably beyond, he was a luminary, a man who had been painted by Sargent. If he'd said his name was Zeus, and he had taken a fancy to pootling round a museum, few would have questioned his sanity.

Edward "Ned" Robinson was the Director of the Met, its head curator. His empire, for it was nothing less, encompassed tens of thousands of works of art that dated from the present, back through to the classical world of Rome, of Greece and of Egypt and beyond. The Met housed one of the greatest collections of art treasures in the world and he was its head. Yet, despite such responsibility, despite his erudition, he was never less than awed by the good fortune that allowed him to be in such a beautiful repository of culture.

The entrance hall always made him feel as if fortune had decided it wasn't enough that he be good-looking, intelligent and rich; the imposing columns reached skyward with the sort of lofty ambition one might associate with a particularly senior Greek deity's choice of interior decor.

It was a cavernous space, with colonnades at the north, west and south ends, providing access to the galleries that were constantly expanding as the museum's collection grew. And, thanks to Robinson, it was growing rapidly. Donations were continually arriving, either in the form of financial endowments, or works of art bequeathed by the many multi-millionaires like Frick, Morgan or Altman, who were all keen to establish a legacy for themselves, beyond a reputation for having acquired vast amounts of money.

Robinson spied a group standing near the information desk. On his way towards them he continually stopped to say a 'good morning' to visitors or staff. He had time for them all. The group up ahead comprised a man around his age, but a little shorter and certainly not aging so well. With him was a beautiful young woman with auburn hair. Beside her was a young girl, who Robinson guessed to be around eleven or twelve. Her face made his heart leap. He could see on it the same rapture that he felt about the Met.

'Flynn, you old so-and-so,' said Robinson, as he approached the group.

'Less of the old, Ned,' replied Flynn, a smile splitting his face. 'I'm younger than you, remember.'

'Mother Nature seems not to have received the telegram, old boy,' laughed Robinson, grasping his old friend's hand and shaking it warmly. He then turned to Bobbie and gave her a kiss on the cheek. 'My word Bobbie, you grow lovelier by the year. Your father must be at his wit's end dealing with your beaus.'

'I always carry a gun, just in case,' said Flynn, one eyebrow raised.

Bobbie laughed and then gestured to Violet Scott.

'And this is Miss Violet,' said Robinson, holding out his hand. Violet immediately held out hers and they shook hands.

'This is Violet, indeed and she is rather excited,' said Bobbie proudly.

'I'm delighted to hear it and you should be excited. I've been coming here for thirty years and I never tire of it. Tell me, Miss Violet, is this your first time here?' asked Robinson.

Violet replied, 'No, I've been a couple of times with...' Then she paused, her voice caught in the back of her throat as she recalled the couple who had adopted her. They had done so only to make her a pawn in a plan to extort money from a rich family. The story had been a *cause celebre* the previous month when she had been kidnapped. Thanks to Bobbie and in no small part to the little girl's courage, the kidnap had a happy outcome, at least until it was revealed who had instigated it. Now Violet was back at the orphanage. Yet, she knew that this was, potentially, not for long. Violet looked up at Bobbie and then said, 'It's the first time with Bobbie.'

Robinson smiled sympathetically, 'Well, you could have no better companion to accompany you, Violet. Bobbie has spent almost as much time here as I have.'

Bobbie and Flynn laughed at this. Flynn nodded and said, 'It's true. I think she could be a tour guide here. In fact...'

'Thank you, daddy, but I like what I am doing,' said Bobbie, taking hold of her father's arm.

This brought a roll of the eye from Flynn, who was less than ecstatic at the idea of his daughter working on the crime desk of a newspaper. On the back of her recent run of scoops, Thornton Kent had extended her responsibilities at the *New York American* to include crime. She would spend three days a week on her old position, Obituaries and two days supporting the rather uninspiring Ade Barton on the crime desk.

Flynn was conflicted about this. The idea of his only child facing any danger was the greatest fear in his life. Yet, how could he not feel a fatherly pride at her achievement. Pride and fear make for uncomfortable companions in a father. Locking her away in a convent had its appeal, but this was unlikely to succeed.

'Are you sure you don't want to be a tour guide, Bobbie?' asked Robinson playfully. 'I'd love to have you here. But I can see how covering crime in the city might be a lot more exciting.'

'And dangerous,' added Flynn, sullenly. A memory of his daughter standing beside a woman holding a grenade flashed in his mind, causing him to shiver involuntarily.

This made Robinson chuckle, but he understood a father's fear for his daughter. It was a universal feeling and even he felt it for the young woman that he'd known since she was a child. The young girl, Violet, reminded him of Bobbie, a lot. There was a keen intelligence in her eyes and a strong streak of independence in her stance if he read her right.

'I do have a nice treat for you though. I have arranged for you to meet the members of the art department at eleven,' announced Robinson. He addressed this to Violet, as this was all for her. Violet's eyes lit up at this. This brought a smile to

Robinson's face. He said, 'I hoped that might impress you. So where to first? I have an hour and a half free, so I am in your hands, then I must leave you.'

'I love the paintings and then I'd like to see William the Hippo,' said Violet, 'and then, maybe after lunch, the Greek gallery. That's your area isn't it, Mr Robinson?'

'Mr Robinson is an expert across everything, trust me,' said Bobbie.

'That's an exaggeration, young lady,' laughed Robinson and meant it. He was renowned for his humility when, in reality, he was as learned on art as he was on classical history, which he had studied at Harvard.

'No, it's not,' said Bobbie and her father in unison. Robinson ignored them and smiled down at Violet.

'The art galleries it shall be,' said Robinson. 'And who knows? Perhaps I can re-join you in Greece.'

'That would be wonderful,' grinned Bobbie, turning towards the great staircase that led to the galleries.

Half an hour later they arrived in a gallery with masterpieces from the Dutch school. On one side were portraits of men and women, wearing black with ruffled white collars. On the other were *trompe d'oeils,* cold looking landscapes and still life paintings, depicted with almost photographic accuracy.

Robinson pointed to one of the paintings depicting fruit beginning to rot.

'If you look closely here, you see the hint of corruption. Of rot. The painter is telling us that life is short. Everything must die.'

'Not too soon I hope,' added Flynn, sardonically.

'Possibly more your area than mine,' laughed Robinson.

The group made their way towards one particular portrait of a middle-aged man. He wore a large black beret and, with the dark background and his impassive expression, the overwhelming sense was of melancholy.

'Strange to think, Flynn old fellow, that he's younger than us in this portrait. Fifty-four, I believe,' said Robinson.

Flynn edged closer to the painting and studied it intently.

'Looks so much older,' he concurred. 'He's eight years younger than me.'

'Ten in my case,' said Robinson. 'Then again, Rembrandt had lived a hard life by then. You can see it etched on his face.'

Violet was curious. She turned to Robinson and asked what he meant. The Museum Director glanced at Bobbie, who nodded. It was not as if Violet, in her eleven years on the planet, had not seen the harder side of life herself.

'Well, many of his children died soon after they were born and he was constantly facing financial ruin,' he explained.

'I see what you mean,' said Violet, peering up at the jowly features of the artist.

'You are very fortunate that you've been able to see this painting. We are lending it to the Rijksmuseum in Amsterdam for a few months. It and few of our other Dutch masters will be coming off the walls later and will head off to The Netherlands. It's quite something that we're in a position to lend. Once upon a time, we had our begging bowl out, to other museums, for exhibits.'

'You've come a long way Ned, that's for sure,' said Flynn, clapping him on the back.

'Anyway, shall we go and see William the hippo?' asked Robinson, conscious that he did not have as much time to spend with his old friend Flynn and the detective's family, as he would have liked.

A chorus of assent greeted the suggestion and off they set to locate the blue hippopotamus, a tiny figurine figure made in ancient Egypt around two thousand B.C. The ceramic figure had been acquired in 1917 and it had quickly become one of its most popular exhibits, especially with children.

As they made their way towards the Egyptian galleries, a uniformed security guard hurried over towards the group. As he was far from young, he had to catch his breath when he arrived.

'Hello Desmond, what brings you here?' asked Robinson, in a friendly tone, but his face looked concerned. There was something in Desmond's manner that suggested a serious matter had arisen, requiring his attention.

'Mr Robinson,' said Desmond, 'may I have a moment of your time?' Robinson stopped and turned towards the security guard. The guard glanced at the group and then back to the Museum Director. 'If we could speak in private.' His face wasn't just serious, it was grave, noted Bobbie.

Robinson smiled to the group and said, 'Excuse me, duty calls.'

He and the guard spoke in low voices for a minute. When Robinson turned back to the group his face was drawn, almost pale.

'I'm afraid something rather urgent has come up and I shall have to cut short our tour, Violet. I am so sorry.' Robinson bowed to the young girl. Then he addressed his old friend. 'Flynn this matter is rather serious and I hope you don't mind joining me.'

'Of course, Ned,' said Flynn, who could see that something serious must have happened, if Robinson's changed appearance was anything to go by.

Robinson nodded to Flynn, then he glanced towards Bobbie and Violet once more, 'Please, forgive me. Violet you could have no better tour guide believe me.'

He shook hands with Violet and gave Bobbie another peck on the cheek. This had a finality to it, which suggested that she would not see her father's friend for the rest of the day.

Events were to prove otherwise.

2

'That's a pity,' said Bobbie, fighting a desire to chase after her father and find out what was going on. The thought, immediately, made her feel guilty. She was with Violet. It was their day together. Yet it had taken root now. And it was a problem, for it risked making her feel resentful towards the little girl that she had now bonded with.

There was a reason she had bonded with Violet and the precocious imp quickly reminded Bobbie of why they had taken to one another.

'Shall we follow them?' said Violet.

Bobbie's head snapped down towards the child. To her delight, she could see the curiosity burning in her eyes.

'Yes,' said Bobbie. 'Let's.'

Once they saw that Flynn and Robinson were a safe enough distance away, they immediately set off behind them. They went through a door that indicated the direction to other galleries.

'I wonder where they're going,' said Bobbie.

'Let's hurry. We don't want them out of sight for too long,' pointed out Violet, as the two men disappeared through the door.

'We don't want to get too close,' reminded Bobbie.

'We don't want to lose them either,' countered the prodigy. It was a good point and Bobbie soon found herself breaking into a gentle jog. She was joined by Violet. 'Besides which,' added Violet, 'if they see us, we can say we were heading towards William the Hippo.'

Bobbie had to congratulate Violet on this idea. It was true. They were, broadly, going in that direction. One of the galleries, mentioned on the sign, was Ancient Egypt. They went through the doors and found that the two men were heading downstairs. They stepped back for a few moments to avoid being seen, before re-joining their pursuit.

'They're still heading in the direction of Ancient Egypt,' said Bobbie. 'That's a stroke of luck.'

The two men, both in their sixties, were walking at quite a clip, which forced the two young women to pick up the pace too. It was proving quite an effort.

'How old is your dad anyway?' asked Violet, who was breathing a little more heavily now.

'Sixty-two going on twenty-one.'

'Gosh, I thought he was older,' said Violet, which probably sounded more unkind than she had meant.

Bobbie laughed at this and replied, 'I suppose he does look a little older than that. It must be a hard life doing what he does.'

They stopped speaking for a few moments, partly to catch their breath and partly to stop and check where the two men had gone as they had dropped out of sight briefly. Violet spotted them heading through another set of doors.

'Definitely Ancient Egypt,' said the child, as she set off after them, followed by Bobbie.

They went through the doors, into a hall full of Egyptian artefacts. Glass cases displayed all manner of pottery and hieroglyphics, dating back two thousand years, or more. Under any other circumstances, Bobbie and Violet would have been fascinated, but their blood was up now, the hunt was on.

'It must be fairly bad for Mr Robinson to pull daddy away like that,' mused Bobbie.

'You don't think there's been a murder?' said Violet, rather too excitedly for Bobbie's liking. It reminded her, too much, of another little girl she knew once, with auburn hair and a policeman for a father.

'I hope not,' said Bobbie, but she wasn't sure she was convincing herself, never mind the child. It was an odd feeling, she acknowledged. She hated the idea of someone losing their life and she scolded herself for the feeling of excitement coursing through her veins. This was one of the many paradoxes she had to deal with, in her desire to work on the crime desk. For her to be able to do what she did, what she most detested had to occur. Bobbie wondered if she would ever be able to reconcile her emotions on this. She hoped not. In an ideal world no one would be hurt. Surely, this was what everyone should wish for.

'That's a problem,' said Bobbie, stopping both herself and Violet, as they were halfway along the cavernous room. Her father and Mr Robinson had stopped to talk with two security guards.

'Something has happened in this section. Look, they're stopping everyone from entering,' said Violet. The security guards had stopped members of the public proceeding further and nothing in the instructions, being given out by Robinson, suggested that this policy was going to change soon. Moments later, they were forced to duck behind an upright sarcophagus, as the Museum Director turned around and began to gesture to the rest of the room.

'Looks like they want to close this room too. Must be serious,' said Bobbie before flashing Violet a warning look that read "don't-say-it" in any language.

'Maybe we should leave,' said Violet.

'The museum?' replied Bobbie, a little disappointed.

'No silly, this room,' retorted Violet. 'There must be other ways we can get to find out what's going on.'

That's the spirit, thought Bobbie. She said, 'Let's go outside and head around the building to the back entrance. Have you that booklet with the plan of the building, Violet?'

Violet took out a small book, from her handbag, and began to leaf through it. In the background they could hear one of the security guards announcing to disappointed visitors, that the room would have to close. The two young women immediately turned and headed for the doors that they had just come through.

Back out in the corridor, Violet showed Bobbie the page with the relevant part of the floor plan.

'I can't see another entrance to this part of the building, either through a gallery or outside.'

Bobbie pointed to a large door at the back and nodded, 'I see what you mean. This is probably where the exhibits arrive. I'm not sure we would get through there.'

This was a bit of a problem. They needed a better idea. Then inspiration struck Bobbie.

'Mr Robinson had promised to introduce us to the painting conservation staff. Perhaps, if we go there, we can find a way out that leads us to the Egyptian section. I'm pretty sure a lot of this building is off limits to the public but may connect with other galleries.'

'We weren't due to meet them until eleven,' pointed out Violet.

'We can arrive early. I'm sure they won't mind,' said Bobbie, hopefully.

They headed down to the central hall and made for the information desk, to find out where they should go for the conservation section of the building. The man behind the counter called over a security guard, to help direct them to where they wanted to go.

They followed the security guard, a man in his mid-fifties, with a moustache that Mark Twain would have envied. As they walked with him, they found out his name was Larry. He led them down a narrow corridor that was off limits to the public and then up a much less grand staircase to the first floor.

'It's the last door on the end,' said Larry. 'Do you want me to come with you?'

'No, you've been very kind Larry,' said Bobbie, if rather surly, she thought.

Larry left them and they made their way down to a door marked 'Art Department'.

'Here goes,' said Bobbie, with a reassuring smile to Violet. She rapped the door a couple of times. This was greeted with silence initially and then they heard a chair scraping along the ground. A few moments later the door opened to reveal a man who was tall and thin, with half-moon spectacles, who could have been anywhere between fifty and seventy.

'Professor Pearson?' asked Bobbie.

The man frowned and said distractedly, 'Yes,' before adding rather oddly, given Bobbie had just addressed him by his name, 'Are you lost?' He looked more lost than they did, a characteristic peculiar to academics.

'No, we've come to see you,' replied Bobbie. 'Mr Robinson arranged this if you remember. I'm sorry but I think we are a little early.'

Pearson continued to look bemused by their appearance. Then a shaft of light clearly appeared to cut through the gloom, for he rolled his eyes and nodded.

'Yes, I seem to remember Robinson saying something about some visitors, as if we didn't have enough to do today with the loan. Well, you're here now. Best come in. Find a seat,' said Pearson distractedly.

Although the room was surprisingly large, this was easier said than done. It was not so much an office, as a long, thin, high-ceilinged room with a table running along the centre. Either side of it was an almost endless set of drawers. It was well lit, as the window bent around acting almost as a skylight. The table had a few mini easels, as well as flat mats, for the conservators, to assist with their work on the paintings in their care.

Bobbie looked around and could not find anything resembling a chair. This was noticed by Pearson, who then pulled out a couple of stools, from under the long table.

'I suppose these will have to do,' he said, unenthusiastically. 'If you take a seat here, I shall look for Miss Mason. She can tell you a little about what we do. I don't know where she has disappeared off to.'

With that, Pearson turned and walked to the far end of the room, passing a painting on an easel that looked very much like a Sargent portrait, to Bobbie's eyes. So much for security, she thought. Curious, Bobbie hopped down from the stool and walked towards it. It was a portrait of a young woman with Sargent's elegant signature in the corner. What Bobbie would have given to be captured on canvas by the great man.

Violet, meanwhile, was intrigued by a small painting on a wooden board. There was a microscope, of sorts, hovering over one section of the painting. Bobbie joined Violet to study it.

'It looks like it's pre-Renaissance,' said Bobbie.

'It is,' said a woman's voice, from just behind them. 'Well spotted.'

Bobbie and Violet turned around, to see a young woman enter the room. She was probably no older than thirty with brown hair cut in a stylish bob style, which contrasted with her rather plain tweed skirt and an old jumper, that had more holes than a golf course. If her intention was to distract from her good looks it was a noble failure.

'I'm Sarah Mason, and you must be Miss Flynn and Violet. Mr Robinson mentioned you would be coming. Is Mr Flynn here too?' asked Miss Mason, looking around.

Bobbie smiled ruefully and replied, 'He and Mr Robinson were called away on an urgent matter, so I have a feeling he won't be able to join us.'

Miss Mason smiled and walked over to join them and said, 'Well, just us girls then.' Bobbie decided that she liked Miss Mason and one look at Violet suggested the young girl was of a similar view.

'I'll take you on a tour of our department. It's quite quiet today, so you've come at a good time,' said Miss Mason. Then she glanced at Bobbie and said, 'You obviously know a little about art.'

'I love this museum. I've been coming for years,' replied Bobbie trying not to sound big-headed.

'And you Violet? Do you like art?' asked Miss Mason.

'Yes,' said Violet excitedly. 'I've been here a few times. Not so many as Bobbie though.'

'Very good, well, why don't we start here with the tools of the trade,' said Miss Mason, pointing to a row of brushes laid out neatly on the table as well as some palette knives, magnifying glasses and around a dozen bottles containing various colours of liquid. 'Now what do you know about art conservation?'

'Nothing,' chorused Bobbie and Violet with a smile. 'I've never seen anything like this before,' added Bobbie.

3

Inspector Flynn had never seen anything like this before either, as he stared down at the murder victim. The dead body belonged to a man; he was lying in a sarcophagus. The corpse was not of the usual sort to be found in a sarcophagus. He was not young, but certainly not two thousand years old. There was also an absence of bandages, which led Flynn and Edward Robinson to conclude that the murder victim was neither an Egyptian nor a long dead Pharaoh.

'His name is Nick Coletti, I believe,' said Robinson. 'He's been a security guard with us for the last few months, perhaps longer.'

Flynn leaned over the sarcophagus, which was lying horizontally on the ground and studied the dead man. Then he turned to his old friend and asked the question uppermost in his mind.

'What is that anyway?'

He was referring to the object sticking out of the, now, former guard.

'That, Flynn, is a khopesh. It was perhaps the deadliest weapon to come out of ancient Egypt. This particular khopesh probably dates back a few thousand years or more.'

'I imagine then, it has the blood of many men already,' observed Flynn.

'Unquestionably,' replied Robinson, who could barely tear his eyes away from the awful sight of his former security guard. In truth, his interest also had a professional tinge too, as this was the first, and only, time he would ever see how such a famous weapon would actually be deployed in real life. He felt a tinge of guilt at the prospect of photographing Nick Coletti's unintended contribution to scholarship as it might be deemed in poor taste. To rid himself of such un-Christian thoughts, Robinson decided a quick lecture was in order, to explain more about the museum artefact that had been used to such deadly purpose.

'The khopesh, as I was saying, dates back at least eighteen hundred years before the birth of Christ. You can't really see it,' said Robinson, pausing for a moment to compose himself, as he stared down at Coletti's surprised face and then the blade that was half-buried in the chest of the security guard, 'but the shape of the blade is like a question mark. In fact, the word "khopesh" means "foreleg of an animal," similar to the English word "dogleg". It was used at close combat as a secondary weapon. It's a little like an axe or short sword and we believe it's purpose was to put the finishing blows on an enemy.'

'Close combat you say?' said Flynn sharply.

'Yes,' replied Robinson, with a frown. He could read what Flynn was thinking. 'Are you suggesting that he knew his killer?'

Like Robinson, Flynn could barely tear his eyes away from the grisly sight. He nodded in response to Robinson's comment and then replied, 'I won't assume anything yet, but that would appear to be the most likely explanation.'

Reluctantly, Flynn touched the face of Coletti. It was ice cold although the degree of rigor was not so advanced. The guard had been dead for at least eight hours, in Flynn's estimation. It was interesting to note that the sarcophagus had delayed the usual onset of decomposition, so the smell around the dead body was less pronounced, thankfully.

'If you could ask your people to close over the sarcophagus with gloved hands, we'll call in our forensic man and a medical examiner.'

Robinson disappeared for a few minutes, leaving Flynn alone in a room full of sarcophagi, and the murdered man. Despite several decades of being in the presence of death, he felt a chill that was not solely to do with the cool temperature of the room.

His friend returned to lead Flynn away from the museum equivalent of a morgue, towards the conservation department offices.

'I don't know about you, Flynn, but I need a coffee. I've seen many dead bodies in my time...' said Robinson, leaving the rest of the sentence unsaid.

'But not many that were killed in the last twenty-four hours I'll bet,' finished Flynn, with a grim smile.

They entered a large office, where three men were sat at desks, all of which had large microscopes and various tools of the trade. The oldest of the three men immediately rose to his feet and went towards Robinson.

'This is a terrible business Ned,' said the man.

'Flynn, may I introduce Professor William Ormond. He is the curator for Ancient Egypt and is also our Chief Conservator for Objects Conservation. William this is Inspector Flynn, an old friend from Harvard.'

Ormond was of a similar age to Flynn. He was tall, slender, with round spectacles and untidy grey hair and a tweed suit that had seen better days, and those were from the last century. You didn't have to be Sherlock Holmes to guess he worked in a museum. His accent might have passed for English.

'Pleased to meet you Professor Ormond,' said Flynn. 'Yes, it's a terrible business. I hope we can make sense of it soon. Do you have a telephone in the department I can use?'

Ormond nodded and said, 'let me show you, Inspector.'

'I shall request some coffees,' added Robinson, as the two men headed towards a door at the far end of the room.

As Ormond and Flynn walked into a second office, with walls banked by cupboards and storage drawers, the professor asked the question uppermost in his mind.

'Inspector, what will become of the khopesh?'

Flynn was slightly taken aback by the question. This was the murder weapon and it would have to be subject to the same forensic examination as any murder weapon would be.

'Well, we will have to fingerprint the weapon. And all of you, I might add so that we may exclude your prints from the investigation.'

'But will the weapon have to leave the museum?'

'Yes, I imagine it will, Professor,' replied Flynn. He could see the pained expression on the conservator's face. 'Why do you ask?'

'It's just that the weapon is four thousand years old and in a fragile state,' said Ormond. Flynn glanced towards the old conservator. I doubt Mr Coletti would agree with you on that, thought Flynn, but kept his counsel. Instead, he tried to reassure Ormond.

'I'm sorry, but we must take the khopesh, as it is evidence. It will be returned to the museum and I can assure you it will be treated with utmost care.'

This went some way to appeasing Ormond, but he was still not happy about the risks involved. Like many academics, he seemed to live for things long dead.

'If I may, I will provide some notes on its care, while the police department hold onto it.'

'That would be very welcome,' replied Flynn. 'Now, I need to call in some of my colleagues. Do you have a home address for Coletti?'

Two minutes later, Ormond handed Flynn a piece of paper, with the address of the dead nightwatchman. Then, he showed Flynn the phone and how to dial out to the police. Soon, a familiar, if not entirely welcome, voice came on the line. It was Lieutenant Grimm at Midtown North. A careerist with no obvious nose for detective work. Flynn rated him as an administrator, but he sensed that he was neither liked, nor appreciated, by the men who reported to him in the squad room.

'Hello, is that you Grimm? It's Flynn. I'm at the Metropolitan Museum. There's been a murder. Can you send along Johnson from Forensics, as well as Nolan? Can you and Yeats go to an address I will give you. The Museum Director is a friend of mine, so I intend handling this personally.'

This news was greeted with a mixture of delight and the usual flattery, from the ambitious Grimm who liked to lay it on thick when the occasion demanded.

'I'm sure you'll show the young bucks how it's done, sir and have the murder cleared up in no time.'

'Let's hope,' said Flynn, keen to get off the line.

A minute later he was back in the main office. Robinson had returned and there was a very welcome tray of coffee cups containing steaming-hot, black coffee.

'Flynn, rather remiss of me, I haven't introduced you to the other members of the department. William, will you do the honours?'

Ormond gestured to the first man, who looked to be in his forties. He was dark-haired, with an impressive beard, that might have qualified him to lead a regiment in the Confederate army, sixty year earlier. Like Ormond, the man had the slightly distracted air of an academic.

'Inspector Flynn, this is my Senior Conservator, Albert Weeks, how long have you been with us Albert?'

'Fifteen years, in June,' said Weeks. He held out his hand to Flynn. It was a little cold and clammy to touch.

'And this is my Assistant Conservator, Thomas Hudson. Tom's been with us seven years,' said Ormond.

'Nine,' corrected Hudson with a smile. He, too, shook Flynn's hand. Hudson appeared a little more like a typical member of the public. He was almost as tall as the rather lanky Ormond but had the build of a quarterback. Like Robinson, he was fair-haired and he also had a beard, but it was well-groomed. Flynn put his age at around thirty-five or a little more. He wondered if he was modelling himself on the Museum Director. He certainly made more of an effort on his appearance than his two colleagues.

'Who found the body?' asked Flynn.

'That was me,' said Hudson, stepping forward. 'Every month I examine the major artefacts like the sarcophagi. We need to make sure there are no signs of rotting or damage from exposure to the public.'

'So, this was a scheduled check?' asked Flynn.

'It was. I have a schedule I can show you. There are so many artefacts under our supervision, it takes a month to two months to examine them all.' He grinned at this, and added, 'A conservator's work is never done.'

'I'm sure it isn't,' said Flynn, with the ghost of a smile. 'And yes, I would like to see the schedule that you have for this. Would it be fair to say that this schedule would only be known to you?' pressed Flynn.

'Not just myself. The other team members too. It's posted up in our office.'

'Thanks, it all sounds very efficient,' said Flynn, trying to keep the hint of surprise from his voice, that such a bookish bunch of men could organise themselves with something approximating efficiency.

Robinson beamed at this and replied, 'I doubt there's a finer antiquities conservation team, in the world, than these men.'

Flynn smiled at his friend who was obviously very proud of his team. What he could not say to his friend, however, was that, for the moment, all three men were the first names on his list of suspects for the murder of Nick Coletti.

4

Miss Mason was proving to be such a fascinating guide, to the area of art conservation and restoration, that both Bobbie and Violet soon found their interest in what had happened in the Ancient Egypt gallery waning a little. But not entirely.

After half an hour of explaining the rudiments of conservation, Miss Mason showed them her latest project. They followed her over to a painting of a man wearing a black doublet. The expression on the man's face suggested he regretted not choosing a larger size of jacket. Bobbie suspected it dated back to the seventeenth or eighteenth century.

'This is a portrait by one of my favourite artists, Anthony Van Dyck. He was a Flemish artist, from what we would call Belgium now. He was very much in demand with the seventeenth century royalty. He painted this while he was still in his teens.'

Violet peered closely at the paintwork, too awed to speak.

'So, what are you doing with this painting?' asked Bobbie.

'I've removed the varnish that they used a century ago. It was making the painting look yellow. If you look up at the top right section of the painting you can see how different the colour seems compared to the rest. I shall remove that now while you watch and then apply some new varnish,' replied Miss Mason.

'Why do they varnish paintings?' asked Violet.

'To protect them,' said Miss Mason. 'It acts like a thin pane of glass but, over time, it begins to discolour, so we need to strip it away and put a new coat on. It's a painstaking process. We must be so careful to avoid damaging the painting underneath. Would you like to have a go, Violet?'

Violet was shocked by the request. She glanced towards Bobbie for support. This made Miss Mason smile. She said, 'Don't worry, I'll show you what to do. I do need to get this done now, as this painting will join a few of the others going out on loan.'

She put some gloves on her hands and sat down in front of the painting. Dabbing a bit of cotton wool into a small bowl of white spirit she gently dabbed a section of the painting. Then she held the cotton wool up to show her guests. It was stained grey by the dirt and grime that had accumulated over the previous century.

'I'll leave that to dry a little then apply the new varnish after lunch. Are you sure you wouldn't like to try doing this. We have a couple of paintings, over there, which I am to work on this week.'

The two paintings in question were small landscape studies from the American Hudson school.

'The artists would have made these quickly, before bringing them back to their studio to work on something a little larger, to say to say the least,' explained Miss Mason.

Another half hour flew by, as both Violet and then Bobbie took turns, under Miss Mason's supervision, to remove some of the grime-stained varnish. While they worked, Miss Mason talked about how she had come to be an assistant conservator in the museum.

'I wanted to be an artist and even went to Accademia di Belle Arti in Florence. When the war broke out, I returned home without finishing my degree. I suppose that didn't matter so much, as I didn't need a degree to be a fine artist, but there was not much demand for art by classically trained artists. Now everyone wants art that you could do Violet. That was not for me, so I managed to get a job here. At least in the museum, there is a need for someone who can mix their own paints and preserve the wonderful art of yesteryear.'

Towards the end of their scheduled time with Miss Mason, a younger man appeared. He was about Miss Mason's age and, to Bobbie's eyes, was not the worst looking man she would see that week although he did give the appearance that he suspected you were thinking just that. Bobbie, immediately, wondered if he and Miss Mason were an item. Both were a similar age and each very good-looking.

'Who are these people?' snapped the young man at Miss Mason. This, instantly, disabused Bobbie of any notion that their delightful host could be in any way interested in such a rude man. On second appraisal, Bobbie could sense the insecurity in the rather shrill tone of his voice.

'Hello Ross,' said Miss Mason, 'I've missed you.' Nothing in her voice suggested this was remotely the case. 'Miss Flynn, Violet, may I introduce my colleague...'

'Your boss,' said the new arrival.

'My boss, Roscoe Meredith. Ross, this is Miss Bobbie Flynn and Violet. Mr Robinson asked that I show them our work in the art conservation department.'

'Mr Robinson, you say,' said Meredith. His manner softened a little. 'Well, I suppose if it came from him.' He turned to Bobbie and, for the first time, it occurred to him that she was someone that he really should have tried harder to make a good first impression upon. However, women have a way of showing by look, by gesture and most certainly by word, that they find a man's presence unwelcome. Meredith was under no illusion from looking at Bobbie that any chance of recovering her good impression had disappeared forever.

'I hope you have a pleasant morning Miss Flynn, Violet.' With this he turned around and walked away.

The ladies watched him leave in silence before Bobbie turned to Miss Mason with a raised eyebrow.

'A charming man, don't you think?' said Miss Mason dryly.

'Indeed. I'm positively swept off my feet,' replied Bobbie with a conspiratorial grin.

Miss Mason erupted into laughter at this, as did Violet, who was clearly seething at the rudeness of Meredith. Any thoughts she would have shared on that topic were swiftly silenced by a look from Bobbie.

'What are your plans now?' asked Miss Mason, glancing up at the clock on the wall. The time was 12:15.

'We were going to have some lunch and then see if the Egyptian Gallery has re-opened,' said Bobbie.

A frown crossed Miss Mason's forehead. She looked quizzically at Bobbie and asked, 'What do you mean?'

Violet decided that she could supply the information as well as Bobbie.

'Inspector Flynn and Mr Robinson were called away earlier on an urgent matter. And when we went down to the gallery to find William the Hippo, it had been closed off for the moment.'

'I wonder why?' mused Miss Mason.

'So did we,' said Bobbie. 'It's certainly a mystery and, if my father is there, I suspect it may not be good news.'

'You say your father is a policeman?' replied Miss Mason.

Bobbie filled in the art conservator on who her father was and his role in the NYPD. By the time she had finished, the atmosphere had certainly changed, as all three considered just how serious matters were, down in the Egyptian Gallery.

When Bobbie had finished, Miss Mason looked bemused, but then she smiled. She said to Bobbie and Violet, 'Look, my day is pretty light at the moment, I don't usually come in on a Sunday. It will get busier this afternoon when we start moving pictures for the loan. Why don't we go for an early lunch and then try to find out what's going on?'

This was met with immediate approval. They left the museum via a side door for the office and conservation staff and headed to a little restaurant that was often used by employees of the museum.

They found a table by the window and ordered a light lunch. As they chatted about the extraordinary adventure, involving Violet's kidnap, the little restaurant soon began to fill up. Miss Mason recognised one of the men who entered in a small group. It was Professor Ormond the Egyptologist.

'Oh, that's a surprise,' said Miss Mason when she spied him. 'They don't usually come here.'

'Who?' asked Violet, looking towards the door.

'The older gentleman in the tweed suit and those two other men. That's Professor Ormond with his team from Egyptology, Professor Weeks and Professor Hudson. They might be able to tell us what's going on. I'll pop over to them and see if they can tell me anything.'

The three men were shown to a table and quickly ordered lunch. Miss Mason nodded to Bobbie and Violet and quickly made her way over to the table with the three men. All three immediately rose to their feet, which was instantly met by Miss Mason asking them to sit.

'What brings you gentlemen in today?' asked Miss Mason.

'Well, we were going to celebrate Hudson leaving for a dig next week, near Cairo. However, there's been a rather tragic incident,' replied Ormond.

As there were quite a few people in the restaurant, it was difficult for Bobbie and Violet to make out what was being said in the group. It was clear the three men were both animated and, to Bobbie's eyes, a little upset.

The arrival of the food to Bobbie's table saw Miss Mason return. She sat down and leaned in. With her voice lowered she said, 'This is rather shocking, but it seems one of our nightwatchmen has been murdered.'

'What happened?' asked Bobbie, forgetting for a moment they had a child with them. Miss Mason glanced towards Violet and then her eyes went to Bobbie.

Violet was having none of this, of course.

'Miss Mason, I was kidnapped and escaped. I grew up in Hell's Kitchen and saw things that no girl my age should see. I think I can handle news about a murder.'

Bobbie half-smiled, rolled her eyes and then nodded to Miss Mason.

'I think it best you tell us, or she shall be a pain for the rest of lunchtime.'

'I shall,' confirmed Violet nonchalantly.

'Very well. The murder victim was a security guard named Coletti. I don't know him, myself. Anyway, it appears he was stabbed with an Egyptian sword. They found him hidden in a sarcophagus.'

'Hidden in a sarcophagus,' repeated Violet, in surprise. 'How strange.'

'How awful,' said Bobbie. Then another thought struck her. 'Hidden, you say? I wonder why the murderer did that?'

'Why do you ask that?' said Miss Mason. She seemed surprised by Bobbie's reaction.

Bobbie paused for a few moments, to collect her thoughts. Then she replied slowly, 'It's strange because if you kill someone you wouldn't normally put the dead body in a place that it's likely to be found. Not unless you had a good reason anyway. In this case, I'm not sure where Mr Coletti was killed, but I imagine it was probably near to where he was found. So why hide him in a place where he was likely to be found quickly? I mean, why hide him at all in that case? There must have been some reason to do that.'

'To escape?' suggested Miss Mason.

Bobbie considered this, but it was clear that she was sceptical. Then she explained why.

'He must have been killed last night some time. I doubt there were very many people around in the museum then. Aside from nightwatchmen, are there many people who work late?'

'It depends really,' mused Miss Mason. 'If we have a new exhibition, then you might have deliveries, which means the curators will have to be around. The conservation teams tend not to work very late, but sometimes I will stay until seven or after. A few others too. Not very often though. Tonight, I will be because we have to help with the loan of the paintings to Amsterdam.' Then Miss Mason added with a mischievous smile, 'You seem to know a lot about these things. Did your father teach you this?'

Violet interjected, 'Bobbie's a real good detective too. She found out who kidnapped me and she solved the murders of George Rankin and Matt Nicholls.'

This took Miss Mason aback and her eyes widened in amazement.

'Is this true?' laughed Miss Mason.

'Not quite,' said Bobbie modestly.

'Is so,' butted in Violet proudly.

'I had a lot of help on the murders,' replied Bobbie thinking of her unusual English friends, Agatha and Mary Aston. Her mind drifted towards Detective Nolan, but as quickly as his, rather handsome, face entered her mind, she cleared it of him. That would not do. She could never trust him.

'So, you did help solve those crimes?' stated Miss Mason.

'Yes,' confirmed Violet.

'Sort of,' said Bobbie at the same moment, but in a voice that would not have fooled a child.

5

Around fifteen minutes after Flynn had called the Midtown North precinct, four policemen arrived at the museum. Detective Nolan was a young man that Flynn rated highly for his ability, while harbouring suspicions about him, for reasons that had nothing to do with police work. Nolan was, by any standards, a good-looking young man, who any mother would delight in having as a son-in-law. This had not gone entirely unnoticed by Bobbie, or her father for that matter. Flynn suspected that, had Nancy still been alive, she would have earmarked the young detective as potential marriage material for Bobbie.

Flynn was not so much concerned about his daughter's interest in Nolan, although he was, as her interest in police work. He was resolutely against this. He suspected a losing battle awaited him on both counts, but he would go down fighting.

To be fair to Bobbie, she had not expressed any interest in Nolan or, indeed, mentioned him since the successful conclusion of the Rankin / Nicholls murders. As part of this case, she and Nolan had visited a speakeasy one evening, under the guise of a romantic couple. It was in Flynn's nature to wonder just how much this required of their acting abilities. His daughter was a beauty, with distinctive auburn hair. Her looks would certainly have been noticed by the young detective, who Flynn knew to be unmarried.

The arrival of the men from the precinct brought Flynn's thoughts back to their present predicament. Accompanying Nolan was Johnson, the forensics man. He had been with the department for over a decade and he knew his job. Flynn could leave him to get on with the painstaking work of fingerprinting, along with one of the two patrolmen, who Nolan had brought along with him. The other would be used to help take statements from the museum employees, about the dead man.

A brief handshake and an even briefer nod from Flynn, constituted the welcome for Nolan and the new arrivals, followed by a curt, 'This way.'

Flynn led them into the gallery to where the nightwatchman lay dead, in his ancient coffin and told them who the dead man was. Anticipating the next question, Nolan said to Flynn as he gazed at the grisly sight of Coletti, 'The Medical Examiner is on his way.' Then he added, *sotto voce*, 'Doesn't look like suicide.' This was typical of the gallows humour of policemen. It was a self defence mechanism to cope with the shocking reality of man or woman's inhumanity.

'It doesn't,' said Flynn grimly. Then he turned to Johnson and said, 'It's all yours.' Flynn noted with approval that Nolan was wandering around the gallery, looking at the exhibits. This wasn't any desire on the young detective's part to take in a bit of history. He was looking for any signs of a struggle, or hint at how the body might have ended up in its unusual tomb. Flynn went over to join him, along with the patrolman, someone he'd known for many years. His name was Mulcahy.

Mulcahy's reddish hair was slowing bleaching which made starker the reddish skin. He could not have looked more Irish than if he'd necked a bottle of whisky and broke out into song.

'See anything?' asked Flynn, as the two older policemen watched the younger man prowl around the murder scene.

'No,' admitted Nolan. 'No sign of any fight. So, either he wasn't killed here or he knew the killer,' said Nolan, turning to Flynn.

'I agree,' said Flynn. 'Let's leave Johnson to his work. We'll go down to the victim's office. He shared it with other nightwatchmen. I think we'll have to have a few of them come in a bit early, so we can find out who was the last person to see him.'

At this point, they were joined by the Assistant Conservator, Thomas Hudson. He and Nolan sized each other up. They were of a similar age, height and build. The only difference was that Nolan was darker and clean shaven while the fair-haired Hudson was bearded.

'Can you take us to the nightwatchmen's office?' asked Flynn.

'Of course, it's in the basement, near the rear entrance which takes in the new arrivals to the museum. Follow me.'

They walked down a narrow staircase, not accessible to the public, that led to a basement floor. While they were walking down the steps, Nolan wondered if the man they were following had gone over to the war, as he had. More and more he thought about these things. The recent murders of George Rankin and Matt Nicholl had made such thoughts more frequent. Unlike Matt Nicholl, Nolan had readjusted to civilian life, mostly. There were nightmares that he told no one about. No one.

They were his and his alone.

They reached the bottom of the staircase, which led to a very cold part of the museum. The ceilings were high and it felt more like an empty office building than a museum.

'This is where we store the artifacts and works of art which are not on display or about to go on display or loan,' explained Hudson. There were large wooden partitions, rather than rooms. Each with double doors that all had keys.

'Why do you leave the keys in the doors?' asked Nolan.

'Strictly speaking they shouldn't,' said Hudson grimly. 'I'll have a word with Sampson about that.'

'Sampson?' quizzed Nolan.

'The head of security. The keys should be hanging up in the office over there.' Hudson pointed to the office used by security and the nightwatchmen. We'll leave them in the doors for the moment.'

'Can I look?' asked Nolan, who was standing near one of the storage units.

'Sure,' said Hudson and led them across to the nearest storage unit. He opened the door and inside were rows and rows of framed paintings. Nolan nodded to the conservator and they moved to the next unit.

Hudson opened the door to reveal shelves containing wooden crates.

'We keep artifacts from the middle east here. Persian pottery and weapons; the usual,' said Hudson. 'Would you like to see any more of the storage units?'

'No thanks,' replied Flynn. Then he turned to Nolan and said, 'I wonder why they didn't just hide the dead man down here?'

'Yes,' said Nolan. 'It's almost like they wanted Coletti to be discovered.'

Thomas Hudson overheard this remark and exclaimed, 'Why on earth would anyone want to do that?'

'Any number of reasons,' said Flynn, but then, frustratingly, did not elucidate. 'Let's see the office.' Flynn looked around for Nolan who had been over by another storage unit. Nolan was nowhere to be seen. Then a door opened and, much to Flynn's surprise, Nolan reappeared. Flynn stared at Nolan for a few seconds and then said irritably, 'Whenever you're ready, Detective Nolan.'

There was a look on Nolan's face that was hard to decipher, but Flynn was more interested in finding out about security. He turned to Hudson and asked, 'What time do the nightwatchmen arrive?'

'They start work at six in the evening and work through until six the next morning,' said Hudson. 'I think we have around a dozen men. I understand they man the exits and some patrol the building at regular intervals.'

'Have you ever had any thefts?' asked Flynn.

Hudson thought for a minute and replied, 'I would be lying if I said it hadn't happened, but Mr Robinson is more likely to have the detail on that or Mr Sampson.'

'That's the head of security?' said Nolan to Flynn.

'And of the museum stewards and attendants as well,' added Hudson. 'Although the attendants are often just another branch of security. All staff who are not...'

'Educated?" suggested Flynn, with a wry smile.

Hudson did have the grace to smile at this remark, but replied diplomatically, 'A member of the conservatorship or curatorial departments. Mr Sampson usually comes in around lunchtime so I hope he can shed light on any thefts that might have occurred and also poor Mr Coletti.'

Flynn and Hudson walked over to an office that was situated by a large set of doors, which were big enough to allow vans to enter, while Nolan explored the storage units once more. He seemed unusually fascinated by them. Flynn made a mental note to ask him what was on his mind.

The office itself was rather compact. There were three desks, some cabinets and a small stove which, presumably, allowed the nightwatchmen to make coffee, to sustain them during the night.

'We should get Johnson to take fingerprints here too,' said Flynn. 'I'm afraid we will have to seal this office, until he has done this. And we will also have to take fingerprints from all the conservators, Mr Hudson.'

'I understand,' said Hudson with a smile.

Around two in the afternoon, Ron Sampson arrived to find policemen and a dead body in the museum. This was a first for him. He was a tall, lean man in his late thirties with tanned skin and clear blue eyes that seemed to see right through you. Upon his arrival, he was directed to locate Flynn and Nolan who, along with patrolman Mulcahy, were interviewing various members of staff.

He was met by Nolan in the gallery where the dead man had been found and was just in time to see the removal of Coletti from the museum. Two stretcher bearers, accompanied by the medical examiner, passed Nolan and Sampson, before they were able to speak. Sampson decided against looking at the dead body under the white sheet as it passed him, but he did remove his hat. In Nolan's eyes, this was something in his favour.

'Sampson?' asked Nolan when the stretcher bearers had passed by.

'That's me,' drawled Sampson. He was from Texas.

Nolan showed Sampson his badge and said, 'Come with me please.'

Nolan led the Texan to a meeting room used by the conservation departments across the museum. It had been turned into a murder room, of sorts. Inside, at the far end of the room, Mulcahy was interviewing one of Sampson's nightwatchmen, who had been called in early. On the other side of the table, a man was taking the fingerprints of Albert Weeks. Thomas Hudson looked like he was next in line.

Flynn saw Sampson enter the room. He rose from his seat as Sampson approached.

'Sampson?' asked Flynn.

'That's me,' repeated Sampson, a slow smile crossing his face. Even Nolan smiled at this.

'Sit down and tell us about Coletti,' said Flynn.

'Any coffee going?' asked Sampson looking around him.

'I'm sure we can get some,' replied Flynn. 'Now, about Coletti.'

The Texan stretched out his long legs and fixed his eyes on Flynn.

'I hired Coletti last summer. He'd good references from his last job.'

'Where was that?' asked Flynn.

'In Chicago at some bank. I think he'd split from his wife and wanted to come back to New York. He had a New York accent so I guess this was his home.'

'What was he like? Asked Nolan.

'You askin' me if he had any enemies?' said Sampson, the lazy smile reappearing. He seemed remarkably untroubled by the death of one of his staff, notwithstanding the moment of respect he'd shown as the body left the gallery.

'What was he like?' repeated Nolan, not rising to the bait.

'Unpopular, I would say. Not one of my more inspired hires,' said Sampson.

'How so?' probed Nolan.

'Bellyacher. Never happy, always complaining about something or other. No disrespect to him, but he won't be sorely missed. I can see why he became a nightwatchman. Kinda suited his personality. Solitary.'

'Enemies?' asked Nolan, and a ghost of a smile appeared on his lips.

'I don't know. I'm not exactly sure who would want to kill a man, least of all Coletti. We don't work sociable hours and he wasn't exactly the life and soul of the party. But that's no reason to kill him either, in my book.'

'I see,' said Flynn. He was troubled by what he heard. If Coletti was in the habit of upsetting people, it suggested that enemies were many and friends were few. This meant they would have to cast the net wide. A feeling of fatigue began to invade his body. Was he too old for this game? Perhaps he should have left this to the younger men? Nolan was almost ready and, notwithstanding his doubts around Lieutenant Grimm and Captain O'Riordan, they had experience, but were still relatively young.

The head of security seemed to sense his fatigue, thought Flynn. Those eyes were as penetrating as he'd ever seen. It made Flynn wonder if the man before him had ever been a cop.

'Were you ever in the police?' asked Flynn suddenly. Sampson's face fell momentarily which pleased the old inspector. He had.

'Eight years in San Antonio Police Department,' said Sampson.

'What happened?' asked Flynn, genuinely interested. Oddly, he quite liked the Texan.

'Let's just say I blotted my copybook,' replied Sampson. Flynn said nothing to this, which made the Texan smile. He would have used similar techniques as a detective. He nodded an acknowledgement to Flynn and then added, 'I didn't get on with my captain. Tended to arrest folk on the basis of their skin colour, rather than evidence.'

'What happened?' asked Flynn, unable to control his curiosity.

'He went to hospital. I went to jail.'

6

Bobbie, Violet and Miss Mason returned to the museum soon after one in the afternoon, following a quick lunch. News of the murder had reached the art conservation department by the time they had returned. Fletcher Pearson, the head of the department, was handling the matter, with all the unruffled serenity of a guard dog spotting a cat. He was walking hither and thither, talking to himself distractedly and refusing all appeals from Roscoe Meredith to sit and calm down. Miss Mason and her guests arrived to find the state of fussing at a very high level.

Meredith, needing something or someone to take his irritation out on, inevitably chose Miss Mason.

'I think Miss Mason, it might be time for our guests to return to the gallery. Quite apart from the fact that there is a dead man in the Egyptian Rooms, I'm sure that you have work to do.'

Before Miss Mason could reply to the man she reported to, Bobbie stepped forward and spoke. Her youth and evident good looks were enough to halt, momentarily, Professor Pearson's efforts to wear out a hole in the carpet.

'Miss Mason has been a wonderful host to us and I shall certainly be telling Mr Robinson this. Mr Robinson, I should add, is an old family friend. My father has known him for forty years. I'm sure he will be very interested to hear how our morning went.'

Miss Mason tried not to cheer, but she also felt it best to avoid the eyes of either Bobbie or Violet, lest her delight at the sterling defence that Bobbie had neatly turned into an attack, should be observed by her ill-mannered boss.

The short speech by Bobbie seemed to pull Professor Pearson back into reality. He said, 'Thank you young lady. That is very kind of you. Well done, Sarah. Well done.'

Meredith looked as if he had caught a sensitive part of his anatomy in the door. He turned puce, which as the name suggests, is not quite akin to looking heroic, or dashingly romantic. It's more likely to radiate a sense of constipation in the beholder. Any hint of Meredith's good looks had all but vanished, beneath this air of supressed rage.

Bobbie turned to Miss Mason and said, 'Thank you Miss Mason, for an informative and enjoyable morning. What do you say, Violet?'

Violet was no dummy when it came to understanding the mysterious manners, the undercurrents and the overflows of adult interaction. In short, she made Machiavelli's ideal Prince seem like a credulous cretin and she played her part to perfection. She ran over to Miss Mason and hugged her closely. Then, with tears almost dripping from every word she cried, 'Thank you, Miss Mason. This was the best day of my life.'

Given that her life had involved two sets of parents who had either, or were prepared to, abandon her or kidnap her, this was probably not setting the bar as high as it might have seemed to the men, at that moment. Bobbie held her breath for a moment, fearful that Violet had overplayed her hand.

There was no doubt in her mind that the little imp was gaming the situation, and then some.

Pearson clapped his hands; he seemed almost on the point of tears himself. He exclaimed, 'Oh well done Miss Mason.'

This was greeted with a modest smile from the heroine of the day, a sharp look in Bobbie's direction from Violet, who was still clinging to the art restorer, as if her very life depended on it. Bobbie made a chopping gesture with her hand which made the young girl disengage.

'I think we can find our own way out,' said Bobbie. She smiled to Miss Mason and Professor Pearson, but made a point of glaring at Meredith, whose colour had turned to crimson.

'Let me come with you,' said Miss Mason.

'No please, Miss Mason. We wouldn't hear of it and you clearly have your work to do.'

With that, Bobbie took Violet's hand and with a nod made her way to the door. As they walked along the corridor, Bobbie turned to Violet and grinned.

'Remind me not to get on the wrong side of you.'

Violet smiled and then she felt a wave of emotion, which made her turn away from Bobbie. Nothing would ever come between her and Bobbie. She realised for the hundredth time just how much she adored the young woman holding her hand.

Bobbie misread Violet's sudden turning away from her as curiosity towards a second corridor they had arrived at that branched away from the door that led to the stairwell up to the public part of the museum.

'I wonder where that leads?' asked Bobbie.

'Only one way to find out,' replied Violet, with a tug of Bobbie's hand. This effectively decided them and they set off down the corridor. There were a few doors that they could have tried but tacitly it seemed they preferred to keep going, to see where the corridor may lead.

To another corridor and another stairwell was the simple answer. This corridor was even longer than the one they had just negotiated. They were committed now so they kept on walking. It felt to Bobbie that they were, if her sense of direction did not lie, at the Central Park side of the building. Once more there were doors that they ignored, choosing instead to keep moving onward. There were, at least, some brass nameplates on the doors. They were, it seemed, in the administration part of the building. The only problem they faced now was running into someone, who might question why exactly they were in a part of the museum that palpably they should not be in.

The first people they encountered emerged from a door further behind them. They were too far away to make any comment on the presence of Bobbie and Violet. Onward they marched until they arrived at another stairwell and corridor. It seemed they were lapping around the building. At some point they would have to run into something that enticed them inward, otherwise they risked returning to the point from which they had originally departed.

The next corridor was not quite so long. They set off and it soon became apparent they were in the conservator section, as the first office they passed had a brass name plate with "Antiquities" in block letters.

'We need to be careful now. I think we are close to where my father might have based himself,' said Bobbie.

The corridor had a different feel to it than the others. It seemed wider with a higher ceiling. As they marched along it, voices could be heard from a stairwell, along with footsteps.

'What shall we do?' asked Violet, aware of the sounds from up ahead. Her voice was calm, which was certainly a tonic for Bobbie, whose heart was racing by now. Bobbie stopped at some double doors. She opened them and went inside. It was a cavernous chamber, with what appeared to Bobbie to be storage units. She grabbed Violet's hand and went over to the first one. It was locked.

The noises in the corridor were louder now. Bobbie and Violet ran over to the second unit. It too was locked. They tried the next unit.

The door opened.

They darted inside, just as some men appeared in the chamber. Bobbie recognised her father's voice. He was asking questions of another man, whose voice was unfamiliar.

Violet, meanwhile, was looking around her. The storage unit was full of framed paintings. She saw Bobbie give her a look that read don't-touch-anything in one hundred languages. Violet, for once, complied.

Bobbie and Violet waited as they heard keys rattle and one of the storage units open. Once more, Bobbie's heart was beating rapidly. Violet was smiling nervously back at her. There was little they could do if they were discovered as there was no obvious hiding place. They waited as they heard a second storage unit opening. The group were very close now. Her father's voice echoed around the large storeroom. It would echo even louder if he discovered her inside with Violet, she thought ruefully.

They listened to the voices outside. There was a third man with her father, one whose voice Bobbie knew only too well. Sadly, Violet had recognised the voice too, as her face lit up with a triumphant grin, that Bobbie tried to ignore. In fact, Violet was now making as if she was going to call out to Nolan to join them. Bobbie could not help but supress a chuckle at this. Yet, part of her was rebelling against this. She thought back, as she often had, to that moment a few weeks ago when she saw O'Riordan pass money to Nolan in a shop doorway outside the precinct.

'Would you like to see any more of the storage units?' said the voice that Bobbie did not recognise.

'No thanks,' replied her father. Then she heard him add, 'I wonder why they didn't just hide the dead man down here? The sarcophagi here would have been a much better option.'

'Yes, it's almost like they wanted Coletti to be discovered,' said Nolan.

'Why on earth would anyone want to do that?' said another voice.

Bobbie heard her father say, 'Any number of reasons.'

And then the door opened. Bobbie found herself facing a rather shocked looking Detective Nolan. The young detective stared in shock at Bobbie and then he looked down at Violet.

Violet smiled and waved to Nolan.

Nolan smiled at her, waved and then frowned at Bobbie.

Bobbie's face fell like a hangman at the gallows. She put her finger to her lips and shook her head.

Nolan looked unhappy but nodded. He turned and left the storage unit, shutting the door behind him. Bobbie heard her father say caustically, 'Whenever you're ready Detective Nolan.'

This created further conflict in Bobbie. She felt angry at her father for what he'd said and the way he'd spoken to Nolan, yet she hated herself for feeling sorry for a detective she now believed was 'on the take'.

The door closed leaving Bobbie and Violet alone. Both were silent for a few moments while they listened to the sound of the men walking away. Then they looked at one another and both smiled the smile of relief, rather than humour.

'He's so nice,' said Violet. 'You really should.'

Quite what the eleven-year-old girl had in mind when she said 'should' was not one that Bobbie wanted to investigate, but a bigger part of her than she cared to admit still yearned to be close to Nolan. She shrugged off this feeling and walked over to the door.

It opened again.

Nolan stepped in after a brief look behind him. Once more he looked to Bobbie and to Violet as if he could not quite believe his eyes.

'What on earth are you doing in here?' asked Nolan, in an urgent whisper. It was clear why he was a good detective. He made straight for the point, offering no escape route with his question. However, it's very directness, coupled with her suppressed anger with him for having let her down, at least her idea of him, meant that Bobbie was in no mood for conversation.

'It's a long story and I don't intend telling it to you,' retorted Bobbie. This made both Nolan and Violet look sharply at her. The anger in her eyes was its own warning to Nolan so he said nothing. Instead, he turned to the door and, once more, walked out of the unit.

Violet looked up at Bobbie, her eyes wide. Bobbie was aware of this and could not bring herself to look at the child. However, children in general and this child in particular, are not fools. They can sense tension and there was no question that the air in the storeroom was crackling with it. She frowned and asked the question uppermost in her mind, 'Did you two have an argument or something?' There was no response from Bobbie on this, so Violet persisted. 'This is crazy nuts, Bobbie. He's the berries.'

7

Had they had an argument?

No, was the easy answer and yet even this was loaded, with more meaning than Bobbie cared to admit. It would represent a form of confirmation to Violet that she did harbour feelings towards the detective. Rather than admit even this, Bobbie decided on a more playful answer that was at odds with her mood.

'You have a very vivid imagination,' replied Bobbie.

Violet was too smart to be dismissed so easily. In this regard, she reminded Bobbie of herself, when she was this age. It might have been funny had they not been hiding from her father and a man she was, possibly, in love with, in an art storeroom, during a murder investigation. There were complications aplenty just then and things were only going to get worse.

The words "murder investigation", in her mind, acted as a reminder of why they were there in the first place and sparked Bobbie into action. She said, 'We should get out of here if the coast is clear.'

'Where to?'

Therein lay the dilemma. As ever, she was on the outside looking in on the investigation, with her one avenue, her father, dead set against her ever being involved. The second avenue, Detective Nolan, had been closed off, too. The other great issue she had was Violet. It would be irresponsible of her to pursue any form of inquiry, while accompanied by the young girl.

Aside from the fact that the murder was not something a young child should be exposed to, it was also a risk as, clearly, for there to be a murder, there had also to be a murderer. And this person was still loose and possibly in the museum. It wasn't just possible the murderer was a member of the staff; it was entirely likely. Her father would be thinking on these lines, too.

It was frustrating, to say the least. She needed some inspiration.

And it came from Violet.

'I need to get lost,' said Violet. This produced a shocked look from Bobbie.

'I don't want you to go,' said Bobbie, fearful that the precocious imp had read her mind.

'No, I don't mean that. I mean in the sense of getting lost and being picked up by security and brought down to your father. That way I can find out what's happening in the investigation and then tell you.'

'Father will never tell you what's happening.'

'I know. He can be a bit grumpy,' observed Violet.

'You'd noticed,' laughed Bobbie. 'So what's on your mind?

'Well, we know your father will say nothing, but I'm sure Detective Nolan will.'

'He won't,' said Bobbie.

'I'll tell him it's for you. He likes you. I can tell,' pointed out Violet.

Despite the warm glow at the possibility Nolan did harbour feelings towards her, the idea could not be countenanced. The thought of Detective Nolan helping them was beyond the pale. She wanted him to understand that he was being frozen out. Quite how she planned to communicate this to the young man when she was not speaking to him was a bit of a two-pipe problem as one of her favourite fictional characters might have said.

While she was considering her response to the young girl, which she realised must be to decline her kind offer, Violet, as was her wont, took matters into her own hands.

One moment Bobbie was staring at a painting by Artemisia Gentileschi showing a woman intent on murder, the next she heard the key turning in the lock of the storeroom.

Violet had just locked her in.

Bobbie heard Violet say, 'Sorry, Bobbie. It's the only way.'

'Violet,' shouted Bobbie, half stupefied by what Violet had done, half amused because she did not believe for one second that she would carry the joke too far.

Then she heard the keys being withdrawn from the lock.

'Violet, this isn't funny. Open the door,' said Bobbie, knocking politely, initially, before banging her fists on the door.

Violet ignored her.

In fact, Violet was already moving to a couple of the nearer storage units and removing the keys from their doors. The coast, she had already established, was clear, so having accomplished this task, she sprinted over to the security office. From inside the storage unit, she'd learned from the man speaking to Inspector Flynn that the storeroom keys should have been hanging up there. The office was empty when she reached it. Honestly, she thought, the security in this building is lax. No wonder there's a murderer running around.

She spotted a board on the back wall with keys hanging from it. Darting over to the board she quickly hung the keys up and then exited the office, heading back towards the door that led to the stairs. She could hear Bobbie banging in the door which did provoke a passing sense of guilt. "Passing" was the operative word. The feeling lasted no longer than the blink of a newt's eye.

In fact, she was excited at being herself again.

Naughty.

Bobbie was perfectly safe inside the container and she would soon be released, by which time, she would have extracted more from the "dreamy" detective and given Bobbie a better chance of getting involved. And her, too. It was difficult to avoid the feeling, when listening to Bobbie talk of the cases she had been on, that this was something she wanted to be part of. She had already been involved once, albeit with heart-breaking consequences for her. Yet Violet was also finding out something about being a child.

Youth can weather the storms of life because its very nature is to live in the moment. A young life is too short to wallow in memories and too instinctive to think about the future. Life is a game until that day, sadly, when the game ends and reality begins. For Violet, reality had intruded often in her short life yet, somehow, she had managed to block it out and move on. This was a form of courage, borne of innocence or, perhaps, a rebellion against the idea that this road was the only one she could travel.

The route she was taking, just at that moment, was proving a little longer than she had first envisaged.

Isn't it always the way, when you need a policeman there's never one to be found? Violet's expedition around the bowels of the museum uncovered just such a fact. Door after door yielded nothing except either empty offices, or men at work on some form of restoration or another or, in one particularly lurid episode, an amorous couple, who were old enough to know better.

Finally, fate cast a kindly eye on the young girl's behalf, as she came across a member of the security team who, no doubt, had been called down to the lower ground floor to investigate why a young girl seemed to be wandering lost, around the non-public area of the museum.

Violet ran into the security guard and gave an audible sigh of relief. Before she could speak, he barked at her, 'What do you think you're doing running around here like this? You shouldn't be here. There's been a murder here.' Then he saw who it was and she recognised him.

'Larry,' said Violet.

'Oh, it's you,' came the reply.

Not quite the sympathetic tone that she was expecting, in her guise as a child lost in the confusing world of adults, in need of help. However, she had grown up around people like this. The man's accent was Bronx, the face hard, with more than a suggestion of stupidity.

'I want to confess,' said Violet, deadpan.

This took the security guard back a little. His brow furrowed as he tried to process what Violet had said. It took twenty seconds, which is long enough when you are eleven and have just confessed to a diabolical murder, before the man realised that Violet was probably not being truthful. Then he broke out into a smile.

'You're something, you know that?' said Larry. There was just the ghost of a smile on his face. As they were now back on familiar terms, Violet decided to go for broke.

'Can you please take me to see Inspector Flynn and Detective Nolan?'

The security guard had met Inspector Flynn. The old detective had as flinty an eye as the guard had ever seen. It was if he could read your mind before the thought had even entered it. The guard frowned once more but had to admit defeat.

'This way,' said Larry, 'but you shouldn't be walking around here on your own. A bad thing has happened.'

'I'd heard,' replied Violet.

'Oh,' said Larry, but added nothing to this.

They walked for another few minutes, past several sets of stairs and ended up near to where Violet had started out. It dawned on the little girl that she had simply started out in the wrong direction.

The guard rapped on the door and they entered a large meeting room. There were several people in the room including a few, thankfully, familiar faces.

'Good lord,' said Inspector Flynn, turning away from the group he was standing with which included Edward Robinson. 'What are you doing here?'

'I found her wandering the corridors. She says she wants to confess,' said the security guard.

'That wouldn't surprise me,' said Flynn, looking sternly at Violet. 'It wouldn't surprise me at all.'

Violet held her arms out, in the manner of someone who was to be cuffed. This raised a few smiles around the room and a roll of the eyes from Flynn.

'OK young lady. Where is my daughter?'

'She's locked in a container downstairs, containing lots of paintings,' said Violet, which at least had the benefit of being the truth. She remembered the advice of Mark Twain who suggested always telling the truth, that way you didn't have to remember what you'd said. This was fine as far as it went. It just required that the listener did not probe further on how Bobbie had come to be locked in the unit while Violet had escaped such a fate.

'Why is she locked in and you're not?' asked Flynn. So much for that idea. Time to be creative, thought Violet.

'I went to another room for a look around and someone came along and locked her in,' said Violet. Realising that the ground she was treading on wasn't so much shaky as calamitously likely to collapse, unless she moved things on, she said brightly, 'Do you want me to show you where she is?'

'That would be an idea,' said Flynn. Just as he was about to say something else, he was interrupted by the door opening and a couple of men entering the room.

It was Inspector Grimm followed by Detective Yeats. The younger of the two men looked like a heavyweight boxer, while the older man, Grimm, was short and slightly built, with a buttery manner that Flynn disliked immensely. He was dressed in a tailored suit that emphasised, rather than hid, his size. Timothy Yeats had once been a linebacker for his college until his expulsion from both the team and said college caused by his putting a quarterback into hospital. His *own* quarterback. The young lady at the centre of this particular *menage a trois* had long since become a distant memory.

Inspector Flynn was never a man to stand on ceremony when it came to greetings and introductions. Something on the faces of Grimm and Yeats suggested that they had a story to tell and the clock was ticking on its telling.

'Well?' said Flynn, which was brief even by his high standards.

The two men had clearly rushed to the museum, having been to the building where the dead man had lived.

'We searched Coletti's apartment as you asked,' said Grimm. Then, from a leather bag, he extracted rolled up papers. As Flynn went to take them, Grimm held his hand up. It was then that Flynn realised he was wearing gloves.

'What's on these?' asked Flynn, his eyes flicking towards the rolls in Grimm's hand.

'Floor plans, security details and,' added Grimm, fishing something else from the leather satchel, 'these.'

'Keys,' said Flynn, a frown creasing his forehead. 'Where to?'

'This building,' said Grimm. 'And these plans are for this building too.'

'Meaning?' Asked Flynn.

'Coletti was planning to rob the museum. These plans, and a few other things, tell us he was planning to rob the museum of some Egyptian hippo.'

'William?' exclaimed Edward Robinson. 'That's impossible.'

'Not according to what we have here. The plan must have been for Coletti to let the thieves into the museum,' replied Grimm, turning to Robinson. Grimm was a careerist policeman who had the finely tuned antennae of a well-bred newt, when it came to sensing authority.

'Why kill him then, if he was part of the gang?' asked Nolan, who was a little less impressed by power. The murder seemed incomprehensible to him and even Violet was nodding at this.

'Unless he was not expecting to be found,' suggested Yeats. 'Perhaps he'd already fulfilled his side of the bargain and provided the keys to enter the museum.'

'So, the thieves would have had new keys cut,' said Grimm. 'And then do a little cutting of their own, specifically this man Coletti, out of the deal.'

Nolan shook his head, which is probably never a good idea when your boss has expressed an opinion. Young people eventually learn these things.

'How did he end up inside the sarcophagus. It had to be an inside job and if it was an inside job, then why bother killing Coletti? It doesn't make sense.'

The idea that your boss wasn't making sense certainly landed with Grimm as well as Flynn. The former decided that he would need to have a word with his subordinate to put him wise about making him look like a fool in public. Flynn's conversation with Nolan would cover similar territory, but its tone was likely to be less critical. However, he did recognise it was time to step in to this debate, lest it spiral out of control.

'We need to understand more about what happened. We won't find any answers arguing with each other in here. First things first, if this plan is to be believed, we must deal with a potential robbery this evening.'

'They'll never do it now that Coletti has been discovered,' said Grimm.

Flynn glanced towards Nolan, who looked sceptical about this. His inclination was to trust the young detective's instincts.

Before Flynn could find the middle way between the two views, Edward Robinson spoke up.

'As head of the museum, I have to agree with Inspector Flynn. We do have a potential robbery to deal with on our hands. I think I might need to speak to our insurance company about this and see how they want to deal with this matter.'

'Don't they trust the police?' snapped Grimm towards Robinson. The latter raised a patrician eyebrow at this, but he remained composed.

Even Flynn wasn't sure he would trust the police on this matter. There were a few rotten apples he could think of. For all his petty posturing, he didn't have Grimm down as one of them.

'Of course, we do lieutenant, that goes without saying,' said Robinson, a little tersely, 'but this is out of my hands. We will inform the insurance companies. We have several of them who underwrite our collection. They will all insist on bringing in Dick Devenish to oversee security arrangements.'

'Who in hell is Dick Devenish?' snapped Sampson, taking the words out of the mouths of Grimm and Nolan who were similarly unfamiliar.

Flynn groaned, when he heard the name Devenish.

'Anyone but him,' growled Flynn, in a low, frustrated voice.

'It's out of my hands, Flynn, old boy,' smiled Robinson, sympathetically. However, there was, just the hint of, a smile on his lips. 'You'll be glad to know he lives very close by, so I imagine he can be with us soon. I've been dealing with him on the loan to Amsterdam, he's a good man. He sees things others don't see.'

'Not everyone is looking in the mirror,' snapped Flynn, which made Robinson chuckle.

Grimm frowned and looked towards Flynn, for some sort of enlightenment on the subject of Devenish. However, Flynn was in no mood to explain. He shook his head and simply said to his men, 'You'll see.' Then, as if he had suddenly remembered something important, he turned to Violet, 'Can someone accompany this young lady and release my daughter?'

8

Bobbie was not someone given to any feelings of claustrophobia, normally. However, a room, such as the one she was in, takes on a very different character when you hear keys turning in the lock and then the clank as they are removed. While she was not, quite, angry with Violet, she was certainly feeling a little displeased. Violet would have to understand that she had gone too far. Which is to say, even by Bobbie's high standards, she had gone too far.

As there was nothing much else to do, Bobbie used her time to look at the different paintings that were stored in the room. They were mostly Dutch portraits, which she realised, with some shock, included at least two Rembrandts. There were also a couple of still life paintings, dating back to the seventeenth century. They were technically astonishing, but after five minutes, Bobbie found herself growing a little bored of seeing perfectly depicted misted grapes in a bowl and jolly men and women, always dressed in black.

After exploring the room for a few minutes, she sat down and waited for Violet to return and release her. The only thing that was going to save that young lady from a severe telling off, was if she had some decent intelligence on the progress of the investigation. At this point in time, Bobbie was not considering trying to solve the murder. Her only interest was in covering the story for her newspaper, the *New York American*, which was owned by William Randolph Hearst.

Salvation came ten minutes later as Bobbie heard keys in the door. She leapt to her feet and was met by Violet, who ran into the room and hugged Bobbie. There were tears in her eyes, as she buried her face in Bobbie chest. Bobbie frowned at this as she was not sure whether to believe that they were authentic, or a show for the security guard they'd met before, who looked as if he would rather be anywhere else than here.

'Let's go,' he said finally and Violet immediately let go of Bobbie. She had miraculously regained her composure. This brought a hard stare from Bobbie, which Violet responded to with a grin.

'I've a lot to tell you,' said Violet.

'How much is a lot?' murmured Bobbie, not sure if she was in a mood to laugh, be angry, or forgive. She adopted a tone that would have gained approval from her friend and colleague, Damon Runyon, 'It better be good, sister or you're for the chop.'

'Trust me,' replied Violet.

This was probably the last thing Bobbie was ever going to do with this Satanic little imp. Yet, despite what Violet had done, Bobbie could not help but admire her sheer nerve. There was a lot about this girl she recognised. She was certain her father did too. Her father might even be enjoying a degree of *schadenfreude* over this.

It was as if Fate herself had decided to perform a comic reversal for Bobbie, so that she could understand how it must have been, for a long-suffering father to watch his only child indulge in one dangerous folly after another. And still do so to this day.

They walked down the corridor to the meeting room which Flynn was using as his base for operations. They entered to find her father stooped over the meeting room table, looking at sheets of paper laid out. He glanced up when she entered.

Bobbie, meanwhile, was aware that Nolan was in the room, along with Yeats and another man, that she had not met before, but from his appearance she guessed this was Lieutenant Grimm. Also in the room was a tall, tanned man in his mid-thirties with striking blue eyes. The final person in the room was Edward Robinson.

Bobbie walked into the room, ignoring, Nolan, but giving Yeats a nod and a smile. This was noted by Violet, who frowned and shot a glance towards Nolan. She could see he had noticed this also, but his face registered no emotion.

What was going on with Bobbie?

'The captive is free,' said Flynn sourly.

Bobbie said nothing to this, but half-smiled. Edward Robinson was, a little more, sympathetic.

'What happened,' he asked, concern on his face.

'I was locked in by accident. Violet and I lost our way a bit, after we met Miss Mason in the art conservation department.'

'Well, I'm glad you're back with us,' replied Robinson. 'I hope you both enjoyed your morning.'

'Oh yes, Miss Mason was wonderful,' said Violet enthusiastically.

Bobbie nodded and added, 'She was. Please convey our thanks to her, once more, if you see her Mr Robinson.'

Robinson assured them he would, then he turned, expectantly, to Flynn.

'I shall let you gentlemen get on with your work. Would you mind if Mr Sampson stayed with you, while you plan your response? I can take Bobbie and Violet back up into the museum if you like.'

'I would,' said Flynn, staring at his daughter, meaningfully. Bobbie nodded in response, to acknowledge the message had been received loud and clear.

Once more, eyes fixed ahead to ignore Nolan, Bobbie followed Robinson out of the meeting room, accompanied by Violet. Out in the corridor, away from the ears of her father, Bobbie began to interrogate Robinson on the latest news, related to the murder.

'I see Detective Yeats is there, with Lieutenant Grimm. What brings them along?' asked Bobbie.

Robinson, who was unaware of Bobbie's unusually high disposition towards becoming embroiled in murder cases, answered truthfully, 'It seems that there may be more to the murder than we realised. Mr Coletti may not have been the man we thought he was.'

'Detective Yeats and Lieutenant Grimm found plans for the museum at his home,' prompted Violet helpfully.

'Yes, that's true,' acknowledged Robinson. 'Sadly, it looks as if Coletti was conspiring to rob us.'

'William the Hippo,' added Violet.

'Really?' exclaimed Bobbie, casting a wry glance in the direction of her partner, not so much in crime as detection. 'How can we be sure he was planning to steal this?'

'Oh, it's all written out,' admitted Robinson, guilelessly.

'Really?' repeated Bobbie. This time her tone was less surprise and more scepticism. 'But why would Mr Coletti be killed if he was part of a plan to steal an artefact from the museum.'

'Detective Nolan asked a similar question,' said Robinson, as they emerged into the public part of the museum.

He would, thought Bobbie unsure whether to feel happy that she was on the right track, or unhappy because Detective Nolan was too. Robinson stopped in the main entrance hallway and smiled to his two guests.

'Well, Bobbie, I think you know your way from here. I must go and await my next guest.'

Bobbie was too curious not to ask, 'Anyone interesting?'

'Oh, it's a revolving door today. This one is to do with this terrible business of the robbery. A fellow who works with our insurance company, an investigator, Dick Devenish.'

'Dick Devenish?' said Bobbie. 'What does my father think of Dick coming in?'

Robinson laughed at this and said, 'You sound like you know Mr Devenish.'

'Our paths have crossed before. Interesting man,' said Bobbie in a neutral tone.

Robinson smiled at this and said, 'I think you can guess what your father thinks of this, but my hands are tied. We must inform them of any thefts or, indeed, anything that might lead to a robbery. That's what we are facing now.'

Violet was intensely curious about the new man, but said nothing, hoping someone would expand on who he was. To her relief, Robinson added, 'Well, if you know him, Bobbie, perhaps you both can join me in my office, while we wait for the great man's arrival.'

'Is he a great man?' asked Violet, with a suspicious frown.

'He thinks he is,' replied Bobbie, with a smile.

Twenty minutes later, and several cups of tea from beautiful China crockery that Bobbie declared an intention to steal from Robinson, a secretary announced the arrival of Dick Devenish. Bobbie rolled her eyes, to Robinson's amusement, but Violet was intensely curious by now.

They his voice was heard first before they saw him. He was from Boston if Violet's ear for accents was not lying to her. Definitely upper crust. This was not a man who disliked the sound of his own voice.

The door burst open and Dick Devenish stood framed in the entranceway. He was around six feet tall, very slender, wearing a suit that had been cut to fit his frame. His suit was light grey, to match his eyes, his Homberg, black. He wore a blue shirt with white starched collars and a yellow and black striped tie. His arms were in front of his body, clutching a black cane with a solid silver handle. He wore very light grey leather gloves. Violet had no clue about age, but to her he seemed to be like Detective Nolan, with dark hair and an attractive light tan to his skin.

'Good afternoon, Robinson, I gather someone is being rather naughty at the moment and wanting to steal dear William.'

Then Dick spotted Violet and he pointed his cane at her.

'Is it you young lady? You have a guilty face. Yes, Robinson, I warrant we have the thief here already, I'll be bound.'

Violet erupted into laughter at this and clapped her hands in delight. Bobbie could not stop herself rolling her eyes once more. Robinson, despite the seriousness of the situation, had to smile also.

Devenish fixed his eyes on Bobbie and a slow smile spread across his face.

'Hello Red. Looking as delicious as ever. Have you decided on my marriage proposal yet?'

'What marriage proposal?' laughed Bobbie who turned to a shocked Violet and shook her head slightly.

'How remiss of me. Haven't I asked you?' exclaimed Devenish. 'Is it too late to do so now, Red my darling? By the way, is this scamp your child? You started early if she is.'

'This is Violet, Dick,' said Bobbie.

Devenish strode forward and loomed over Violet, who was still smiling at the new arrival. He made a great play about studying her intently. He seemed to reach a conclusion and asked, 'Ah yes, are you the child that was kidnapped?'

'I was,' confirmed Violet.

'And now you are a thief,' accused Devenish.

'I'm not,' exclaimed Violet, but she was laughing as she said this. So, too, were Bobbie and Robinson.

'Very well,' said Devenish and leaned down towards her, 'But I have my eye on you, young lady. Now, take me to William. No, actually, not William. Take me to the scene of the murder. I may as well solve that particular piece of villainy while I am here. Who may I ask is handling it from our worthy New York Police Department?'

'My dad,' replied Bobbie, drily.

This brought a dramatic grimace from Devenish.

'I see. Should he not be at City Hall or somewhere, decapitating politicians? He'd enjoy that, I'm sure, more than having to skulk around the grimy reality of murder.'

'The Metropolitan Museum is hardly grimy, Devenish,' observed Robinson, a half-smile on his face.

'A mere observation directed towards the degeneracy of the act rather than the hallowed halls of this bastion of silent dignity, of told and untold stories waiting to unfurl like the flags of a long dead victorious army.'

'Shall we go and see my father?' suggested Bobbie, with a heavy sardonic tone.

'Lead on Lady Macbeth, lead on,' replied Devenish, pointing his cane to the doorway.

9

The arrival of Devenish in the meeting room was akin to a whirlwind erupting at a house of cards competition. Having already received their cue from Inspector Flynn, Nolan, Grimm and Yeats were anticipating his arrival with no great enthusiasm. As it turned out their worst fears came nowhere near to the extravagant reality of the ego they were encountering for the first time.

'Inspector Flynn,' roared Devenish, in mock delight as he entered the meeting room, accompanied by Bobbie, Violet and Robinson. 'What a pleasure to see you once more. It's been too long, sir, far too long.'

'Not long enough, Devenish,' snapped Flynn, sulkily.

'Come now Flynn, don't be like that. How many cases have I helped you on?'

'Five.'

'And how many came to a successful conclusion where good triumphed over evil, where justice was served, where the guilty parties now languish in a dark dungeon?'

'Five,' said Flynn, sounding even more like a teenage schoolboy.

'There, you see. We make a great team, you and I, Flynn. Now, please introduce me to these worthy foot soldiers of justice.'

Foot soldiers of justice?

Nolan glanced at Bobbie, who held his eyes for a moment, then looked away. This was disconcerting to Nolan, for he now no longer sensed, but knew, something was wrong. As ever for most men, he had no idea what the offence was, when it was committed or, indeed, how long he would be in the doghouse for.

Introductions were made. The last to shake hands was the Texan head of security, Sampson. The two men eyed each other warily. It was clear to Devenish that the head of security for the Metropolitan was no fool. Something about those clear blue eyes gave one a sense that he could read you, like graffiti on a toilet wall. It was not in the nature of the private investigator to back down from a challenge. There could only be one dominant male in any room that he was in, and he was always intent that it should be him.

'Do I detect a man from the Lone Star State, sir?' asked Devenish.

'You do,' replied Sampson carefully, not sure where this was going.

'And you are the head of security, correct?' continued Devenish, almost as if he was interrogating the Texan.

'I am.'

'Good, can you tell me what arrangements you are going to put in place, to ensure that no robbery takes place?'

'We have the police here for a start, as well as my own security team.'

Sampson had barely answered the question, before the next one was sprung on him from Devenish, 'How many men is that?'

'Six in the evening and another five during the day, as well as the ushers and stewards,' answered Sampson.

'And you can vouch for all of these security men?'

'Hired them myself.'

Devenish spun around in a dramatic fashion and fixed his eyes on Flynn, then the other policemen. His eyes rested on Grimm. The little lieutenant was dressed, as ever, impeccably. Devenish made a show of assessing Grimm and then asked, 'Who is your tailor?'

Grimm was taken aback at first by the question, but then, assuming he was the subject of flattery replied, 'No one, I bought this suit at Macy's.'

'It suits you,' said Devenish, which prompted a proud smile from Grimm, a suppressed chuckle from the two younger detectives and a frown from Flynn, who knew he was making fun of one of his men. While he had little enough sympathy for Grimm, he wasn't about to see him humiliated by this fluffed up popinjay.

'Come with me Beau Brummel, I'll show you the crime scene and then we'll head up to see William the Hippo. The museum shuts in an hour's time so we can start to get our men in place. Sampson, can you get the evening shift to come in earlier?'

'I already sent the message. They'll come in at four-thirty.'

'Good,' said Devenish, trying to reassert control from Flynn. 'Mr Sampson clearly knows what he is doing. Now, let's see if I can help you clear up this murder before the madman strikes again.'

Bobbie looked on amused, waiting to see how her father might react to this latest piece of self-aggrandizement. Watching men wrestling for leadership was something that always entertained her. This was not the first time she had come across Devenish and her father engaged in this primeval struggle for dominance. If she'd been a ringside judge, she would have said they were still pretty evenly matched; the older fighter, cantankerous and fuelled by anger, the younger one, smart, savvy, energetic and fuelled by the sheer amusement of it all.

Flynn was nothing if not a savvy operator himself. He had a few problems on his hands. There was a murder to solve, a theft to prevent and he had one too many chiefs around for his liking.

It was time to reassert some control. He looked at Sampson and said, 'Mr Sampson, can you take Lieutenant Grimm and Detective Yeats to the security office. Furnish them with the names of all the security men, ushers, and stewards. I want a to know everything about them.'

'I say Flynn, you can't seriously believe that this is a conspiracy from within?' exclaimed Robinson.

'Sorry Ned, I can't rule anything out. We'll also need the names of all your curatorial and conservation staff. Anyone who had access to that part of the museum must be able to show where they were last night and I need to know more about how long they've been at the museum, where they were before. Anything that may be material to this investigation. Grimm, you got all that?'

'Yes, sir,' said Grimm, grimly. It was not quite what he wanted, but equally, if there was a robbery looming, it might be better to be in a safe place, in case things got heated. Grimm frowned a little and made some noises about being disappointed about not being around for the real meat of the investigation. This had usually worked at other precincts he'd been stationed at but he sensed, pretty quickly, that Flynn wasn't buying any of his moonshine, so he quickly abandoned this avenue and led Yeats away to begin the background checks on the museum staff.

Then Flynn pointed to the security man, who had originally found Violet.

'Can you take Mr Devenish to the crime scene? I'll join you there in a few minutes, Devenish.'

The two men exited the room which left Flynn alone with Nolan, a patrolman and Robinson as well as Bobbie and Violet.

'This is a terrible business, Flynn. Of all days. I'll have to leave you too, I'm meeting Professor Wouters soon. Is there anything I can do for you?'

Flynn shook his head. He said, in a voice that only hinted at the strain he was feeling, 'We have enough men to deal with any robbery. It's a distraction all the same. We need to find who killed Coletti.' The implication did not need to be spelled out. There was still a murderer free, possibly in the building.

'I shall take my leave of you, for the moment,' said Robinson, and left the room.

Bobbie watched all of this with bated breath and knew what was coming next. She was back in the meeting room, after having been dismissed barely an hour earlier. The second banishment was imminent, she suspected. Her father would not want either herself or Violet involved in a murder case. So, it seemed that the obvious thing to do was to take the initiative.

Why should it only be men who assume control of their, and other people's destinies, she reasoned.

'I'll take Violet away dad,' said Bobbie. 'I'm sure you won't want us around now.'

This provoked several reactions, which ranged from stunned, on the part of Detective Nolan, disappointment from Violet and downright suspicion from both Flynn and Devenish, who knew this particular lady all too well.

'Don't worry,' continued Bobbie, 'we know the way by now. We'll show ourselves out. Come along Violet.'

With that, Bobbie grabbed Violet's hand and led her outside into a corridor they were now very familiar with.

Violet looked up at Bobbie and, to give the child her due, the look of disappointment had given way to a hint of wariness.

'Where exactly are we going, Bobbie?' asked Violet.

'Up to see a certain hippo. That's where they will all end up anyway,' whispered Bobbie.

The corridor echoed to the sound of Violet's laughter which was all too audible for those inside the room. Flynn glanced towards the door his daughter and Violet had, only moments earlier, exited from and, instantly, felt regret that he hadn't asked Nolan to accompany them out of the building. He hoped he wouldn't rue this decision.

Fate, as Flynn had learned over his decades in the NYPD, was a capricious prankster who delighted most in creating twists and turns, rather like talented Irish mystery story writers. The joke would soon be on Bobbie.

10

Amsterdam, The Netherlands 1660

The old man looked at himself in the mirror. He didn't think of himself as old – which of us does, he mused? He looked old, though. A life blessed by genius, not his words, this had been said by others; a life cursed by financial problems, even while his fame was spreading throughout the country and beyond. A life that he had recorded, brushstroke by brushstroke for decades, on canvas.

Each new portrait told its own tale of his life, at that moment. The early self-portraits, when he had made faces, or dressed up in the clothes of historical figures. And now, three dead children, the creditors at his door and age cracking his, once smooth, face apart. He gazed at the jowls of good living and the eyes, those sad, bloodshot, weary eyes that looked to be the result of a lively debate, between insomnia and a bottle of port. But the eyes also had a twinkle of mischief, lurking deep behind, the thin lines of red that streaked through them like a river delta.

He adjusted the black hat. Its jaunty angle belied his mood, though. He was too worn-out to pretend he was anything but exhausted. He looked at the paintbrush in his hand and dipped it into a thick glob of royal umber. He rubbed it in the paint, for a few moments longer than was necessary and then made his first mark on the canvas.

11

The blue ceramic hippo had a funny, dumpy shape that may not have been anatomically accurate for the semi-aquatic mammal yet felt true all the same. The flanks were decorated with the outline of the lotus flowers, buds and leaves. To Violet, it looked like a naughty child had drawn on their parents' pottery, and then dropped it.

A piece appeared to have been chipped off the near forefoot, which made it seem like a badge of honour, a whisper of a story that was two thousand years old. Wide-eyed children gazed in wonder at this tiny yet colossally steadfast presence. Perhaps they recognised that here was something an earlier generation of their peers would have played with and delighted in.

Violet was certainly fascinated by the little ceramic model. Its captivating bright translucent blue green was her favourite colour. She smiled as she saw him and then felt a wave of anger, as she realised that someone wanted to steal the little model. To do so would deprive children, like her, of having a connection with a long dead past. This angered her and she gripped Bobbie's hand a little tighter as she imagined an empty space on the grey plinth.

'How could anyone want to steal him?' asked Violet, as much to herself as to Bobbie.

Bobbie nodded. The little hippo was certainly an oddly beautiful object but, the adult part of her had, perhaps, lost some of that sense of enchantment.

'I'm sure that whoever was planning to do this will stop now,' said Bobbie, in a reassuring voice. She meant it too. The idea, which was extraordinary before the discovery of Coletti's body, now seemed less astonishing, just utterly foolish. Yet, nagging thoughts remained. Why kill Coletti if he was going to be part of the robbery? And why just before the attempt was to be made?

And why this hippo?

Its fame had certainly grown in the few short years since it had arrived as an exhibit in the museum. How much was it worth? Bobbie had no idea. It could either be considered priceless because of its fame as much as its antiquity, or it might be so because it was now in a museum and unlikely ever to be sold.

Who would want it?

Its appeal, for children, could not be doubted. For adults, though? This seemed more of a stretch. Perhaps, a private collector of Egyptian antiquities might want to own such an item. Such people were not beyond dabbling in the black market, for such items. Unquestionably, it was likely that museum staff, over the last half century, might have been bribed to siphon a few artefacts in the direction of rich collectors.

A robbery was a wholly different matter, thought Bobbie. This was another level of risk entirely. It did not seem to her that the image she had, of collectors, quite tallied with master criminals, whose interests were usually financial. Two thoughts struck her about this potential theft.

Either the person behind this was extraordinarily passionate about this artefact, in particular, or the game was very different. William would be kidnapped and a large ransom would be demanded.

Bobbie glanced towards Violet who had so recently suffered a similar fate. Her heart was beating fast now. She adored this child. The kidnapping had brought them together and, in a strange way, she was grateful for this. Was this the plan? It was the only thing that made sense.

Violet was shaking her head, once more, while looking at the tiny hippo. It was in the middle of the gallery on a grey, three-foot-high plinth, enclosed in a glass case. Across from Violet, two children, standing with their parents, were laughing at the sight of the hippo which, in Bobbie's eyes, was the truest way of appreciating it: delight.

The gallery they were in was long and rectangular, with glass display cases running along each wall containing various artefacts, that might have been used in the home, or for hunting. There were two upright sarcophagi, in the middle of the room, further down from where William the hippo was located.

Given that they now knew there was potentially a robbery planned for that night, Bobbie was a little surprised that there was only one security guard in the gallery, along with an usher, who was in the middle, helping an elderly couple. A patrolman walked through the double doors. Bobbie didn't recognise him but then, while she knew many uniformed officers, it was impossible to know them all. Aside from these people, the room was not very crowded, just two families, several students and the elderly couple.

Bobbie glanced up at the clock. It was coming up to quarter to four in the afternoon. The time had certainly flown. The museum would be closing in the next fifteen minutes. This would mean she would have to leave, along with Violet. For a while now, she had been giving thought to how she could extend her stay but, each time an idea came, it perished on the rocks of reality.

To stay would be to put Violet at risk.

Perhaps it was time to go. It was the right thing to do. She would have to leave her father and a certain young Irish-Italian detective, to clear up the murder. She hoped her father would have the good sense to leave dealing with the possible robbery to the security staff and the additional policemen that would have to be drafted in.

'Violet, I think we should go,' Bobbie said, in a despondent voice.

Violet glanced at Bobbie, sideways. Far from looking forlorn, she had a half-smile on her face.

'Are you sure you wouldn't rather stay?' she asked, mischievously.

Bobbie could not help but giggle at this. The young girl could read her like a book. Furthermore, unless Bobbie's guess was wide of the mark, Violet wanted to stick around herself to see what happened.

This was impossible, of course. It really was time to go and leave this to the professionals. Bobbie raised her eyebrow and then took Violet by the hand.

'You're no fun,' complained Violet, but she was smiling as she said it. Despite her disappointment, she knew that there was no way that she could stay. Sister Assumpta would be expecting her back at the orphanage. For how much longer, though? With each passing weekend, with each new experience with Bobbie and her father, the idea of returning to the orphanage, despite her love for Sister Assumpta, grew less appealing. And despite Sister Assumpta's best efforts as a teacher, she missed her old school and the friends she had made there, particularly Lydia Monk.

Bobbie began to lead Violet away from the hippo, towards the thick, wooden, double doors that led to the corridor and the stairs. She turned to take one last look at the hippo. But something was wrong. She saw someone appear from a door at the side that was not for the public.

Their eyes met.

And then, in a matter of seconds, everything changed.

The lights went out, plunging the gallery into darkness.

There were no windows in this gallery, everything was pitch black. Bobbie heard some screams and shouts.

Someone ran past Bobbie.

She heard glass being smashed. Then there was a 'thunk' sound like something had fallen to the ground. Bobbie began to move in the direction of the door with Violet.

And then she crashed into someone. Or someone crashed into her, which sent her spinning around. She collapsed backwards, but someone caught her fall. She tried to disengage herself but could not. There was a strange smell now. What was it?

Violet felt the panic rise within her. But she was with Bobbie and this was enough to stop the wave rising and becoming a terrified scream. And she was terrified. It was not so much the darkness, as the sounds of panic around her and then the sound of the glass smashing,

Someone is taking William, thought Violet, absently.

She and Bobbie had continued walking and had bumped into someone. Her hand was wrenched free from Bobbie's. Then, seconds later, she was thrown to the floor.

Violet cried out, 'Bobbie!' And when there was no answer, she cried out again, a little more frantically. There was still no response.

Kneeling on the ground, with arms outstretched she began to feel around for Bobbie in case she had been dazed by the collision. There was no sign of her. She was feeling panic now, but controlled herself by thinking that Bobbie was around somewhere and that the lights would come on soon.

The screams were growing louder, as were the angry shouts.

'Bobbie,' shouted Violet, once more. This time, there was more than a hint of anxiety in her voice.

There was no answer.

12

Flynn turned back to the men in the room. With him were Detective Nolan and the patrolman. Flynn studied the patrolman. He was not young, yet Flynn could not remember seeing him before. He was an imposing presence – as big as Yeats with a nose that lacked the usual symmetry one expects from nasal architecture. It reminded Flynn of the dog-legged eleventh hole at his club, which he'd never liked.

'Have I seen you around?' asked Flynn, to the patrolman. Always an interesting way of asking a question.

'No sir,' replied Lewis. 'I just joined.'

Lewis looked to be, at least, forty years old.

'The precinct or the NYPD?' pressed Flynn.

'Both, sir,' replied Lewis. 'I was sent by Captain O'Riordan.'

This was not a good sign, as Flynn harboured doubts around the uprightness of that particular detective. More than doubts, he now had some proof that O'Riordan was on the take. Yet, he did not know from whom, but he hoped to find out in due course. That he had been sent by the police captain did not, of course, mean that he was on the take himself, but it was something he would not discount either.

The NYPD and even the Mayor's office, was unquestionably corrupt. The extent of this had yet to be established and probably never would be. Only the previous year, Mayor Hylan and Commissioner Enright had bowed to public pressure to rescind Rule 1984 which effectively gagged police officers from testifying truthfully on corruption, or graft, within the department. Flynn fully supported the rule, many did not.

'What's your name?'

'Lewis, sir.'

Flynn nodded towards the door that Bobbie had exited from, a minute or two earlier.

'Well, Lewis, can you do me a favour? Find your way up to the room with the hippo. I'm sure you can ask someone how to get there. Just stay there until further notice.'

'Yes, sir,' said Lewis. He immediately turned and headed out of the door.

Flynn waited a few moments, as he and Nolan listened to the footsteps of the patrolman, echo up the hallway, then he turned to the young detective and said, 'Have you seen him before?'

Nolan shook his head.

'Can you ring Midtown and ask them about Lewis. I want to know more about who I have around me. There's something strange going on here and I don't much like it. That guy Sampson, too, while you're at it. He's an ex-cop; is he telling the truth?'

Nolan walked to the end of the room to the telephone, to follow up on this request while Flynn stood over the plans of the floor, where the robbery was planned. Criss-crossing his mind were similar questions to those that had troubled Bobbie.

On so many levels, the murder made no sense. It was as if those responsible had deliberately scuppered their own raid. Why would they do this? Had Coletti intended blowing the whistle on them? This made sense from the view of removing him from the picture, but why leave the body in a part of the building where it could be found?

When Nolan returned to Flynn, the old detective had at least one theory he wanted to validate.

'Nolan, speak to Hudson about the team schedule for checking artefacts. How long has that been in place? Could it have been changed for any reason? Was he or someone else meant to find that body in the coffin?'

'Sarcophagus.'

'Don't you start, professor,' growled Flynn. 'I want to know more about that rota for who does what conservation work?'

'Do you think that Hudson deliberately uncovered the body?'

'Who knows? What I do know is that those coffi...sarcophagus things stored dead bodies. They were obviously designed to slow the body's decomposition. So why put the body in there if it was only going to be discovered within a day or two?'

'Perhaps the killer believed the first thing you said that the body would not decay and would not be discovered.'

'Or perhaps they knew it would be discovered and thereby prevent a robbery.'

Nolan thought about this for a few moments and then replied, 'So we have a killer who maybe is not part of the gang but found out there was to be a robbery. For some reason, he kills Coletti because he knows that he is part of the gang. Perhaps he confronted him, they struggled and the killer grabs the first weapon he can find, kills Coletti. He panics and then puts the body in the first place that comes to mind.'

'It would be the first place if you are an Egyptologist,' suggested Flynn, drily but he was impressed by the logic of the young detective.

'Or a woman,' suggested Nolan, ignoring Flynn's comment. 'Coletti might not have been big, but it would have been difficult for a woman to move the body too far.'

Flynn studied the young detective with those penetrating eyes. Nolan didn't flinch from the gaze. The older man shrugged and replied, 'There are no women in this department, though. But, yes, there could be something in that.'

Nolan mused out loud, 'Or the killer was in it with him but, either Coletti had cold feet or, the killer decides he has served his purpose and disposes of him.'

Flynn nodded at this and finished off the thought, 'This would imply that he was a member of, either the security detail that was here that evening or else, he's a member of the conservation team. No one else would have been around that evening.'

'But we've seen that the security records show that each member of the Egyptian conservation team were signed out that night,' said Nolan. 'I checked the records myself when we were down at the office in the basement. Unless, of course, they were faked.'

Flynn flopped down on one of the seats by the meeting table and shook his head. 'We don't have much do we?' he said wearily. He took out a pipe from his pocket and spent the next few minutes puffing reflectively. Smoking a pipe made one seem thoughtful while a cigarette only made one look either agitated or lazy, thought Nolan, who did neither.

The phone ringing in the meeting room, shattered the silence that had descended between the two men. Nolan went over to answer it. He spoke for a few minutes to a person on the other end of the line. When he put the phone receiver back on its holder, he turned to Flynn and said, 'It seems our patrolman was not telling us the full story. He's from Chicago originally and was on the force there. He left last year.'

'He was transferred to us?' asked Flynn.

'No. He left Chicago then came here,' replied Nolan.

Flynn seemed surprised by this. He said in a perplexed tone, 'Why didn't he just ask for a transfer, if he wanted to come to New York?'

'I asked that too, Joe said he'd find out. It doesn't add up,' answered Nolan.

'I can think of a reason why it wouldn't,' murmured Flynn. 'Look, can you go up to that damn hippo? If I know my daughter, that's where she'll have gone. Before you go, what about Sampson? Did they have anything on him?'

'They did. He was in San Antonio Police Department, as he said, for eight years. Then one night he beat up his captain. No reason given on the record. They dismissed him immediately and he did eighteen months for the assault. No word of him after that until he got the job here.'

'I'm not surprised they didn't mention that the captain was a racist. We look after our own don't we,' said Flynn grimly. He paused to think for a moment and then added, 'Ok, look, head upstairs now and keep an eye on things until the museum closes. Are we getting more men down here?'

'Yes, they're on their way,' replied Nolan. Just as he said this, the lights in the room went out. They were in complete darkness as the room had no windows.

'What the hell,' exclaimed Flynn. 'Nolan, get up to the…'

But the door was already opening as he said this.

It shut moments later leaving Flynn alone, in the bleak blackness of the room.

13

Violet screamed.

There seemed nothing else to be done at this point – everyone else was screaming. She sensed people rushing past her trying to get to an exit they couldn't see. Matches were being struck but quite why was beyond Violet because they went out in a matter of seconds.

How long had the lights been out? It felt like an eternity, but Violet realised that it had only been a couple of minutes. Where was Bobbie? More importantly, why wasn't Bobbie calling out for her? It made no sense. And so Violet had screamed. It wasn't for herself. She was afraid for Bobbie.

The lit matches had, at least, informed her that she was near a wall. She held her arms out and walked in the direction of the wall. When she reached it, she sat down. And wept. The sound of crazed shouts and screams would haunt her for a long time. It was the sound of civilisation, of education, of culture breaking down in seconds.

Someone had found the door and opened it. This threw some light into the gallery but not much. It was dark outside so, even though the outside hallway had windows, the amount of light reaching the gallery only made it possible to see some shapes and bright colours. Yet it was reassuring. Trying to detect Bobbie remained impossible and after screaming once,

Violet had given it up as a bad job. This made one, persistent and shrill, screamer even more irritating. A man too. Shameful performance, on his part, thought Violet. It might be better for him if the lights stay off.

A man was shouting that everyone had to stay where they were. This was causing arguments.

And then, as suddenly as they had been cut, the lights came back on. The screamer was mid scream at this point. He stopped and looked around him. Violet caught his eye, but she was too shaken to make her feelings clear on his unmanly reaction. He walked away towards the exit. A policeman stopped him.

The man and then another, who tried to leave, began to argue with the policeman, but he shook his head and was adamant that they stay. It grew heated now and Violet wondered if a fight would break out. Then she glanced towards where she had been standing. She rose to her feet and started to walk quickly, heart racing, towards the plinth that had held the little hippo. The glass was shattered around it and there was no sign of the tiny Egyptian artefact.

And there was no sign of Bobbie.

Violet looked right and left. She looked behind her and then she focussed on the other end of the gallery.

Bobbie was gone.

'Violet!' shouted a voice. A man's voice.

Violet spun around. She saw Detective Nolan run into the gallery. He stopped and stared at her. There was a frown on his face. His eyes flicked towards the plinth and then quickly scanned the room, before returning to Violet.

'Where's Bobbie?' he asked, in a voice that was tight with tension.

Violet shook her head and the tears coursed down her cheeks.

Behind Nolan the crowd were becoming angry and aggressive. Nolan spun around and walked back towards Lewis, who was the policeman manning the door. He clapped his hands to gain everyone's attention.

'Ladies and gentlemen,' he shouted over the growing tumult. 'There has been a robbery in this room. No one can leave until further notice. Step away from the door. All of you.' There was particular emphasis on the last three words.

A few men shouted back, demanding to leave immediately. They were well-dressed and had an air of entitlement about them. Their mood was not helped by Nolan rolling his eyes. Their shouts grew louder.

Nolan pointed behind them, to the shattered case that had once held the hippo.

'One of you may have stolen that object. I want to know who it is,' said Nolan in a loud, clear, but calm, voice. In truth, he did not believe the robber was still in the room, but he needed desperately to buy time for reinforcements to arrive and then he could focus on what was uppermost in his mind.

Finding Bobbie.

This silenced the complaints briefly and then, moments later, more policemen arrived in the gallery which effectively decided the issue. No one was leaving. Nolan immediately strode towards the tearful Violet. There was no need to ask what had happened, as the little girl collapsed into his arms, and cried.

'Bobbie's gone.'

That much was apparent. The question was where. Had she decided to follow the thieves or had they taken her with them as potential leverage, to escape the building? Yet even this seemed strange. The hippo was tiny. Whoever had taken it, could easily have left the building by now.

Nothing added up. Nolan knelt, so that he was face to face with Violet. Behind him he could hear Lewis taking charge of the situation. Had he not been so worried about Bobbie, he might have been impressed by the patrolman's authoritative manner. More people were arriving now. He heard Sampson's voice and then he turned around and saw Dick Devenish arrive. It was turning into a circus.

'Violet, you must tell me everything that happened. Tell me in detail. Take your time. Just go through each moment, step by step. Can you do that for me?' said Nolan. His voice was calm and his composure seemed to cast a spell over the young girl. She took a deep breath and nodded.

Finally, she spoke and said, 'I was with Bobbie over by William. And then the lights went out. I heard screaming and shouts, then someone smashed the glass. I knew they were taking William. Bobbie was still holding my hand, then it was like she was pulled away from me. Someone took her. I know it. She wouldn't have left me like that.'

No, she wouldn't have left just like that. It was inconceivable that she would have followed the robbers and left Violet on her own.

'Violet,' shouted a new voice. It was Flynn. Nolan turned around to see the old inspector moving quickly towards them. 'Why isn't Bobbie here?' asked Flynn. There was a trace of irritation in his voice, but there was no disguising the worry too.

Nolan didn't have time to sugar coat the answer. He was not dealing with the sort of man who wanted some tangential explanation on what might have happened.

'She's missing. Violet believes someone snatched her, during the blackout.'

Flynn's eyes flicked towards the child, who had tears streaming down her face. Violet repeated what she'd said to Nolan. When she had finished. Flynn was about to ask another question, when he stopped himself, following a glance from Nolan.

The young detective was till kneeling in front of Violet. He took her hand and in a very gentle voice he asked, 'Violet, I want you to try and remember what you saw just before the lights went out. Who was standing near you? Do you see them here now?'

Had Flynn not been in such a state of anguish, he would have commended Nolan, for how he was handling the situation. Behind him, he could hear a different approach being used. It was Dick Devenish who was trying to corral an antagonistic crowd to stand in two queues so that statements could be taken. Once more, Flynn had to acknowledge this was not the wrong thing to do. They had to act quickly. Perhaps the reaction of the museum visitors was as much a release of their pent-up fear, as their frustration at having to stay and answer questions from people who suspected them of being robbers.

Violet, thankfully, despite her desolation, was responding in a voice that only periodically broke from suppressing her tears.

Between her sobs, she said, 'There was a family on the other side. I think I see them over there. The girl in the blue dress with the boy.'

Nolan nodded, 'Very good Violet. You're doing well. Who else?'

'That man over there. The fat one,' said Violet.

Violet was not one to sugar-coat things either, apparently. The man was overweight, rather than fat, with a red face that indicated either poor health, or anger, or perhaps both. He certainly did not look to be very happy at that moment, with a set to his face that suggested he would soon be demanding that he speak with the person in charge.

'Very good, Violet. Who else?' said Nolan.

'Those two older women,' came the reply.

It sounded as if she were referring to a couple of spinsters, when in fact the two women in question were probably no older than Bobbie. Both were in their twenties, although the glasses that each were wearing probably added to their age, in Violet's eyes.

'Anyone else?' asked Nolan, trying not to sound impatient.

'There were people behind me, but I didn't see them,' said the young girl. She was visibly growing more composed. 'Perhaps these people will be able to say who was behind me and Bobbie.'

This was Flynn and Nolan's thought too, but each were impressed that the budding young detective had arrived at a similar conclusion. One of the people that Violet had described would, almost certainly, have seen who snatched Bobbie.

'Think, Violet, is there anyone else you saw, perhaps someone who moved away from the exhibit?' Pressed Nolan in a low, calming voice.'

'That policeman was here, the one over there,' said Violet. She was referring to Lewis.

Violet shook her head. Nolan and Flynn exchanged glances. There was little point in trying to push the little girl further. Violet had already given them quite a lot to go on, but there was a limit to how much more they could gain, as she was clearly devastated by Bobbie's disappearance. Nolan put both his hands on Violet's shoulders, looked her in the eye and said, 'You've done well, Violet. Don't worry we'll find her.'

This was meant to reassure the young girl, but it only provoked more tears to stream down her face. She threw her arms around Nolan and he held her for a few moments. He felt her body shake with the anguish she was feeling.

'We'll find her,' said Nolan, as much for himself than for Violet. 'We'll find her.'

14

Darkness.

It enveloped her, pressing on her chest, suffocating.

Finally, a shaft of light appeared. Dim at first and then its shape became more discernible. It was a young woman. She was smiling. Her face was radiant with joy. A man beside her, almost in tears. They were saying something, but she couldn't hear.

The image slowly faded away. Now she was running. She was being chased. No. She was chasing someone. A boy. He tripped and fell and she was laughing. Then he changed into a man. The image faded before she had time to see who it was.

Now she was arguing with a man. Her father. He was older now. She was angry, but not that angry. This happens when you know the other person is probably right. But that wasn't the point.

Now he was standing with a young man. Dark hair, eyes that held your attention. She didn't want her father to be there. She felt guilty about this. He'd always been there for her.

How cruel.

A child appeared. She knew the child. Like her, but not like her. They were chatting. Walking together in the park. Holding hands.

Then darkness descended, but not for long because she was dancing with the young man and, oh boy, she did not want this to end, ever.

It ended.

She was with the child again. They were in a dream. There was a blue hippo before them. Around the hippo were some other children. Adults. She turned around. There was a man in a uniform. He was looking at her. Strangely. Penetrating eyes from beneath his cap.

Blackness again.

And then she woke up to the blackness.

She tried to scream, but there was something stopping her from doing so. She had been gagged with a cotton handkerchief. She tried to remove the gag, but she couldn't.

Her hands were tied behind her. Not tied.

Handcuffed.

Her feet too.

And then she realised with rising horror where she was.

She was inside a box.

A coffin.

15

The Grange, Hampshire: late 1826

Alexander Baring was a man of business, a financier. He was a politician too, although he thought of himself as a statesman. And he was also 1st Baron, Ashburton. In other words, he was a man with many hats, metaphorically speaking. He was wearing one just at that moment. Even though he was inside his own drawing room, it was still cold. A head that had once enjoyed a mane of silken strands, ordered like a row of soldiers on parade, could only boast a few token survivors around each ear. They offered little protection from December weather. Yes, a hat was very useful and he wore it with elan.

He was standing in the drawing room of his estate at The Grange, with half a dozen men, of similar vintage and outlook on life. All had come to celebrate his new acquisition. Not just a painting, nor just a portrait. This was history. It was a chance to be in the presence of greatness. To gaze upon a man who perhaps shared his sense of destiny, if not the same bank balance.

'By Gad, you've done it Ashburton,' said the man standing next to him, who was also holding a glass of port.

'I have,' agreed Baring. And he had.

The two men stood in front of the painting and gazed at it in wonder.

Then Baring turned to his friend and said, 'Strange to think he was about the same age as I am now, when he painted this.'

The two men reflected for a few moments on this revelation, as they studied the features of the man in the painting. He was wearing a black hat at a jaunty angle. It seemed at odds with the rather whimsical, yet sad, look in the eyes of the subject. The jowls around his mouth and the wrinkles which had been so lovingly recreated on the canvas, suggested a man much older than the fifty-two years of the viewer.

'You look much younger, old fellow,' said Baring's friend.

'You're too kind,' said Baring, although he did not disagree. He did look in better shape than the man in the painting. He pointed to the eyes and said, 'Doesn't look very happy, does he?'

'Money troubles,' said the man.

'Wife troubles' suggested Baring. The two men laughed at this, as only men would.

'Both,' said the two men at the same time, which turned merriment onto outright hilarity. Baring reached for the decanter and poured some more port into the two glasses.

16

Violet looked from Nolan to Flynn and felt a little embarrassed for being so emotional. She wiped her eyes and nodded to the two men. The noise around them was growing louder as more men arrived in the gallery. Among the new arrivals to the gallery was Robinson, accompanied by Lieutenant Grimm and Detective Yeats. Robinson went directly to Flynn.

He paused long enough to look at the shattered glass on the plinth, that had once housed the famous little hippo. He seemed to grow paler at the sight.

'It's extraordinary,' said the museum's director in a hushed voice. 'I can't believe it.'

Flynn had almost forgotten about the stolen artefact. He turned to Robinson and said, 'Ned, perhaps you can help us here. Firstly, we need you to go to the visitors over there and calm them down. With the best will in the world, I'm not sure my men are doing that.'

The Museum Director glanced over towards the increasingly hostile crowd. He said, 'Of course, I'll go directly.'

He immediately turned and strode over to where the disgruntled visitors were standing. There was something in his demeanour, his presence, which acted instantly to quell the noise.

'May I have your attention, everyone,' he said in a voice that was raised, but not to the point where he was shouting. It was authoritative enough to command instant silence, even from the patrolmen who had been talking to the visitors.

He paused a moment and slowly scanned the people in front of him. To the visitors, he seemed like the man in charge. He was, of course, under normal circumstances. These were not normal circumstances.

'Ladies and gentlemen and children. My name is Edward Robinson. I am the Museum Director. I apologise for the distress you have experienced over the last ten minutes. As you can see, we have been robbed of one of our most popular and valuable, artefacts. The police are here to find the object and those responsible for its theft. We need your help in this. If you could assist these detectives in their questions, we will try and ensure that you can leave the museum as soon as possible. Unfortunately, no one can leave until the police are satisfied that they have everything they need from you. I will shortly organise for chairs to be brought up to the gallery and we will also provide coffee, tea and some food for you, too, so that your enforced stay can be as comfortable as possible. Thank you.'

Following this, he went over to one of the stewards and said a few words, which Flynn interpreted as being the instructions to bring some chairs.

Flynn knelt, as Nolan had done, next to Violet. He took her hand and said, 'Violet, I promise you we will find Bobbie. In the meantime, I'm going to need you to be a brave girl. Can you do that?'

Violet nodded. She knew what was coming, and despite herself, the tears stung her eyes, once more.

'Can't I stay?' she said and it broke Flynn's heart, to hear her say it.

He shook his head. He tried to smile, but it was never going to be convincing, so he gave up and said, 'Violet, I need to be able to concentrate on finding my little girl. Do you understand? I can't do this if I'm worrying about you.'

Violet nodded at this and knew she was defeated. It wouldn't be fair on Flynn. She smiled weakly and said, 'Find her, Mr Flynn.' Then she looked up at Nolan and said, 'She likes you; you know. I don't know why she's acting so strange. You'll find her, won't you?'

Nolan was too stunned to speak. He nodded and tried to avoid looking at Flynn who would, no doubt, have heard what the little girl had said. Flynn, meanwhile, was motioning for one of the patrolmen to come over to them.

'Mulcahy, I need you to take this young lady. Come with me,' said Flynn taking Violet's hand and leading her and Mulcahy towards the door. As they walked, Flynn explained that Mulcahy was to take her back to the orphanage and Sister Assumpta.

Violet was in despair but, she knew instinctively, that this was too serious for her to be difficult. As much as she wanted to stay and help in some way, Flynn, Nolan and the others needed to focus on finding Bobbie.

Flynn watched Violet disappear from the gallery and then he turned and went back to Nolan, who was prowling around the plinth.

'Thoughts?' asked Flynn.

Nolan's eyes stayed on the plinth, for a few seconds, before shifting to Flynn. He frowned briefly and then said, 'They've taken Miss Flynn as insurance. That means they are still in the building and so is the artefact. I think it must be some of the museum staff. How else would they have known to take Miss Flynn? They must have linked her with you.'

Flynn nodded in agreement. The inspector seemed to age a decade in a matter of minutes. And no wonder. The implications, of what had happened, were now becoming clear to Flynn, as they had to Nolan.

'I shall have to let Grimm take over, for the moment. We'll need O'Riordan here too. I don't care if it's his day off.'

Nolan said nothing to this. The look on Flynn's face said everything he needed to know.

'Find her,' whispered Flynn.

Before Nolan could respond, a familiar voice cut through the air, as it usually did. It was Devenish.

'So, the devils have taken William, have they?' he said, his handmade shoes, tip toeing through the shattered glass towards the empty plinth. 'Sampson has a lot of explaining to do. First a dead body and now this. Yes, what sort of security system do they have here anyway? What are your thoughts, gentlemen?'

Flynn and Nolan exchanged glances and then the inspector turned to face Devenish.

'They've taken Bobbie,' said Flynn.

For a moment, the only sound in the room, was the murmur of voices from the museum visitors and the policemen. Devenish's face grew serious, immediately. His eyes flicked between Flynn and Nolan. Then he nodded.

'That puts a different complexion on things,' he said. 'They'll use her as a bargaining tool if things grow sticky.'

'We know.'

Then Devenish turned towards Grimm, then back to Flynn.

'What's he like? He'll have to take over now.'

'We know,' said Flynn, without enthusiasm. 'I'm going to get Captain O'Riordan here. It's his day off.'

'O'Riordan,' repeated Devenish, with even less enthusiasm than Flynn had shown for Grimm. 'Can't we do better than that?'

Flynn was thinking the same but could hardly say so. He motioned with his head towards Nolan and then nodded to Devenish. 'I'll still be here and you two can work together on this. I'll keep Grimm and O'Riordan off your back. Take Lewis with you. My men can deal with these good folk. You can organise the search of the museum.'

As Flynn said this, the doors to the gallery opened and several men trooped in carrying chairs for the dozen or so people who were being questioned. Robinson was helping them carry the chairs. When he had dropped off the two, he had been carrying, he came over to join Flynn and Nolan.

'Can I get you anything?' asked Robinson.

'We'll need your staff to man the exits and ask people to show what's in their bags and pockets,' said Flynn.

'That's already happening,' replied Robinson. 'There'll be a few objections, no doubt, but we'll make sure that no one leaves with William through the front door.'

'Can you spare any men to help us search for Bobbie?'

'Of course. How many do you need?'

'At least half a dozen men, Ned. Sorry, I know it's a lot to ask.'

'Nonsense. I'll see to it now,' replied Robinson. 'The men meet you down at the basement meeting room in a few minutes. One more thing, I shall have to leave you for an hour. I'm to meet Wouters from the Rijksmuseum, but I'll be back around five thirty.'

'Of course,' said Flynn. Robinson departed immediately to organise the search party.

'I'll go and speak to Grimm,' said Flynn. 'Wait here for a minute and then we'll head down to the meeting room.'

After the old detective left them, the two younger men eyed each other up.

'It looks like he trusts you, Nolan,' said Devenish.

'Looks like he trusts you too,' replied Nolan. There was just a hint of wonder in Nolan's voice, which visibly amused Devenish, much to the young detective's irritation.

'You seem surprised. Don't be deceived by appearances, Nolan. I'm not the fool you think I am,' said Devenish, holding his arms out and smiling.

'No, you're a suspect,' replied Nolan. He wasn't smiling.

17

Five minutes after Flynn had handed over control of the robbery and kidnapping to Grimm, he met with Nolan, Devenish, Lewis and half a dozen stewards and security men, in the meeting room. There was little point in varnishing the truth. He went straight to why they were all there.

'Gentlemen,' began Flynn, his face set like a boxer moments before the bell rings, 'My daughter was in the gallery upstairs when the robbery took place. We believe she was abducted while the small artefact was stolen. Your job, until further notice, is to find my daughter. I will give a reward for the man that finds her. I suggest that you split up into pairs. Detective Nolan and Mr Devenish will each be accompanied by someone who is familiar with the museum. They will search the downstairs galleries. Lewis you will take three men and search the upstairs galleries. Report back here at five thirty.'

The time was now four fifty.

Flynn pointed to one of the security men, 'You and I will search the conservation departments and the basement area with the storage units. Is everyone clear on what they must do?'

There were nods from around the table. The men immediately set off for the places they had been allocated. Flynn turned to the security man.

'I'm Inspector Flynn,' he said. 'I don't think we've been introduced.'

'Barnes,' replied the security guard. 'Larry Barnes.' Flynn judged him to be around fifty years of age, tanned skin, slightly built, but there was a sense of power, emanating from his wiry frame.

They headed out of the door.

'How long have you been with the museum?'

'Five months,' replied Barnes. 'Never seen anything like this before.'

They walked along the corridor and stopped at one of the doors as there were voices inside. Flynn knocked and then entered. Albert Weeks and Tom Hudson looked up from their desks. They both had grave expressions.

'Hello gentlemen,' said Flynn. 'I'm not interrupting anything?'

'No, Inspector Flynn, not at all,' said Weeks. 'We were just discussing the robbery. It's extraordinary really. Who would do such a thing? They can't hope to sell William.'

'They might want to ransom him,' pointed out Flynn, scanning the office for potential places that Bobbie might have been hidden. Hudson stroked his beard and followed Flynn's gaze. There was a door to at the end of the office. Flynn pointed to it and asked, 'Where does that lead?'

Hudson rose from his seat and said, 'Let me show you.' He looked at Flynn strangely, as if he was surprised that they might be considered suspects for the robbery. Flynn wasn't sure if they knew about Bobbie but decided not to explain why he wanted to see where the door led.

Hudson opened the door and switched on the light for the room. It was a storeroom containing banks of drawers. Bobbie was not here.

'Thanks,' said Flynn curtly. 'I'll leave you to your work.'

Out in the corridor, he said, 'Before we go to the basement storage, maybe we should go over to the Art Conservation section. Bobbie was there earlier. How do we get there?'

'This way,' said Barnes.

Flynn was rather relieved that Barnes wasn't the talkative type. He was in no mood for small talk and yet, at the same time, he realised that he could not stop being a cop, just because it was his daughter who was involved.

'Five months, you say. Where were you before?' asked Flynn.

'Night work at a factory,' came the reply. 'Six years and then they laid me off.'

'Why was that?'

'They made shells for artillery. Not many wars going on now,' replied Barnes.

Flynn stopped himself in time from saying "thank the Lord". It might have been considered a little insensitive, to a man that relied on war for his job.

They seemed to have made a circuit of the museum, when they arrived at a corridor where a young woman was standing, talking to a tall man, with a tweed jacket. Talking was perhaps an understatement. The discussion was heated by any standards. The man was jabbing a finger perilously close to the young woman's chest. He stopped himself, just as Flynn and the security man appeared. They both turned around and seemed like two frightened deer in the headlights of a car. Or two children caught with their hands in the biscuit tin.

Flynn kept heading towards them and introduced himself.

'I'm Inspector Flynn. Doubtless you've heard about the theft.'

'Yes, Inspector Flynn, we were just discussing what had happened. My name is Roscoe Meredith and this is Sarah Mason.'

Miss Mason eyed Flynn and then said, 'Are you related to Bobbie, by any chance?'

Flynn's eyes widened at this, 'Have you seen her?'

'Well, yes, earlier today. We were with Bobbie and Violet,' explained Miss Mason, but she could see the frantic look on Flynn's face. She frowned and asked, 'Is something wrong?'

Flynn nodded, but asked instead, 'When did you last see her?'

'They left us around 2:30pm. We didn't see them after that. What's happened?'

'Do you mind if we go through your offices? We're looking for Bobbie. She's missing.'

'Of course,' said Meredith. He stepped forward and opened the nearest door to reveal another office. Flynn stepped inside with the other men to conduct a quick search.

'Bobbie was here earlier,' said Miss Mason, following the men in. 'I showed them all about the restoration of pictures, but tell me, is Violet OK?'

'Yes,' replied Flynn. 'She's shaken of course. She and Bobbie were by the exhibit when the robbery occurred. Speaking of which, where were you when the lights went out?'

Flynn was looking around the room. Unlike some parts of the museum, which did not have any windows, as some galleries were marooned in the middle of others, this room had very high windows, to allow a lot of light through. They would have been a lot less affected by the sudden absence of electric lights.

Meredith took over from Miss Mason, clearly keen to disassociate himself, or their department, from anything remotely resembling involvement in the theft. Also, to Flynn's mind, he looked like a man who wanted people to know he was in charge. It was there in the stance, the voice that was a decibel or two louder than it needed to be. Flynn had no time for such men. But right now, he needed help.

'We were here working. Miss Mason was removing varnish from this panel and I was finalising the inventory of paintings we are lending to the Rijksmuseum.'

Professor Pearson, who Bobbie had met earlier, peeked from behind a door having heard the voices from his office.

'Professor Pearson, this is Inspector Flynn. He's here about the robbery.'

Pearson appeared agitated, 'We've only just heard. How terrible. I hope no one has been hurt, of all the days for this happen.'

The only people who will be hurt are the ones that have taken my daughter, thought Flynn. A wave of fear, mixed with hatred, surged through his body. Where was Bobbie? He needed to think straight and focus. Yet, the anxiety was overpowering him, clouding his mind, sharpening his senses, but in a way that heightened his growing sense of dread.

'Professor Pearson is head curator of Art,' explained Meredith. There was just a hint of sourness in his voice, noted Flynn. Pearson was old and seemed a little befuddled by the world, while Meredith was younger, unquestionably good-looking. Ambition radiated from every pore. Flynn wondered how much this was a show, for the attention of the attractive Miss Mason.

Pearson and Flynn shook hands. If ever a man gave the impression of an absent-minded professor, Flynn was looking at him. He seemed more agitated than the two younger people, who were on his staff.

'We are here to conduct a search of your department,' said Flynn, keen to move quickly. He was in no mood to be diplomatic. The response from Pearson was a curious blend of outrage and confusion. Before this combination could be given a voice, Miss Mason interjected.

'Professor, the young woman you met earlier, Bobbie, is missing. The police will need to search everywhere, thoroughly.'

Flynn nodded a thanks to Miss Mason, for heading off a distracting outburst at the last minute.

'How terrible,' said Pearson and appeared to mean it. 'Please, search anywhere you need to. Miss Mason, could you help in this?'

Miss Mason took the men around in a tour that resembled, very much, the one she had done with Bobbie and Violet earlier. It did not last as long and the result was disappointing. There was nowhere that Bobbie could have been hidden.

Flynn thanked the conservation team and they left the offices, to head down to the basement. Flynn's mind was racing, with the possibilities of what could have happened to his daughter. That she could have been abducted, from the gallery, was possible only if the person doing so knew who she was and how to make the quickest possible exit. They would have had to have done this almost on the spur of the moment, which would make it unlikely they had been able to spirit her away from the museum itself.

Flynn was working on the assumption that Bobbie had been targeted as potential leverage if the thieves were caught. Added to this was a new thought. Had Bobbie recognised who had stolen the artefact? Had she seen someone, just before the lights went out? The more he thought about this, the more he became certain of it.

The theft was almost certainly an inside job.

But who?

18

Bobbie moved her body left and right. There was no question about it. She was in a coffin. Her mind was still a little hazy from the drug that they had used on her, after she had been grabbed. If only she had put up more of a fight. She stopped herself from going too far down that route of reproach. She was trapped, that much was clear. She had no hope of escape. That, too, was evident. What frustrated her most was not knowing for how long she had been unconscious.

Think Bobbie.

She felt nauseous. This was either the fear or it meant that chloroform had been used on her. The more her head cleared, the more she felt the headache. Yes, it had to have been chloroform.

She tried to remember how long the effects of the drug lasted. She remembered Violet saying that when she had been kidnapped the previous month by Renat the Russian and Bugsy McDaid, they had put something over her mouth. She'd woken up around fifteen minutes later. Bobbie could remember a handkerchief being used, to cover her nose and mouth. The smell had been vile. Bobbie decided that something similar must have happened to her.

If she allowed fifteen to twenty minutes for her unconsciousness, it meant that she was in the museum. If it was a coffin then it was likely to be a sarcophagus. Then with a feeling of horror, she thought it might even be the same one that had recently housed Coletti. Why this should have horrified her, even more, she could not say. It was irrational because it hardly made her situation any more perilous.

She tried to remember what had happened. It felt, a little, as if it was the morning after the night before and the night before had been a legendary drinking occasion. She felt ill and her mind was dodging from memory to memory, like a pickpocket escaping a policeman. She couldn't get her thoughts to stay still and focus on one thing at a time.

She had been with Violet.

Violet.

What had happened to the little girl?

Had she been taken also? Was she trapped too? Bobbie felt tears sting her eyes, once more, as she imagined the terror Violet must have felt when the lights went out, when she had been separated from Bobbie and when she realised that Bobbie was missing. The horror of this, at least, had the beneficial side effect of halting the random images that had flooded her mind and helped her to focus once more.

She was alive, but trapped, almost certainly in a sarcophagus.

She had been witness to a robbery.

The robbery. William.

She and Violet had started to walk away from the hippo. She was going to take Violet home. It wasn't fair on her father that she should remain while the investigation of the murder was underway and there was the risk, reality as it turned out, of a robbery about to occur. Then she had heard something and she turned around.

She'd seen someone.

Try as she might, she could not see the person anymore. It was as if the face, the body had been erased. It was a man. He was wearing a uniform. That much she was sure of. She'd thought it odd to see him. But why? Who was it? Given what had happened, it was almost certainly, someone connected to the robbery.

Who?

She felt like screaming once more. This time, bizarrely, it was not because of her situation. Her memory was letting her down. Her body too. She felt sick. The bile was rising within her. Images flooded her head once more and she fought hard to try and focus. But it's difficult to concentrate when your head is pounding. She began to shiver violently as the shock of her situation, combined with the aftereffects of the chloroform, began to take hold.

Any hope of seeing the face was abandoned for the moment.

Her focus now was on surviving.

Yet, her distress was now growing, as another thought loomed large in her mind. How much air was contained in this small compartment. Was the wood porous enough to allow it to come in. Whether it was her anxiety or, more worryingly, the lack of air, the sense that the sarcophagus was growing evermore stuffy was not simply her imagination.

She was running out of air.

And then, incredibly, she heard banging on a door nearby and then someone shouting.

19

Flynn was now fighting hard to stop the growing sense of alarm taking over. He left the Art Conservation department, with a sense that finding his daughter, in such a large building, would make finding a needle in a haystack a breeze, by comparison. They had a lot of men on the task, but each minute that passed increased his sense that she was in danger.

Such fears were never going to lie unspoken in Flynn's head when he could vent them in the corridor. He did so forcefully as soon as he had distanced himself sufficiently from any office likely to hear him. Then he turned to Barnes, the security man accompanying him on the search.

'Sorry, Barnes,' said Flynn ruefully. 'I should show more control.'

'I understand, sir,' said Barnes. 'To the basement?'

'Yes,' came the reply. 'I want to go to the storeroom that has Egyptian artefacts first. Do you know where that is?'

'I do,' answered Barnes. 'There are some of those coffins down there.'

'Good. We'll look there first. Lead the way. I'm getting lost in this damn warren.'

They proceeded down the corridor to the stairwell. Flynn took the stairs two at a time, belying his request for Barnes to lead. The news that there were sarcophagi had given Flynn renewed hope of finding Bobbie.

They reached the corridor, with Flynn now jogging towards the double doors that led to the storage units.

They were locked.

Frantically, Flynn turned to Barnes. The security man held up some keys, which brought a flood of relief to Flynn. He decided not to urge the man to hurry, when he began to flick through the keys to find the right one.

Finally, key found, the door was opened. They marched into the storage area and made for the office where the keys to the storage units were held. Barnes led the way this time as, it was clear to Flynn, there was little point in him exhausting himself. He could only be as quick as Barnes who was plodding along.

'Which one?' asked Flynn, indicating the storage units.

Barnes pointed to the last unit, before ducking into the office to retrieve the key. Flynn headed over to the unit to wait for Barnes. When he reached the door the tension and the fear was unbearable. His heart was racing now and he was almost faint with worry. To release some of the tension, he banged on the door and shouted 'Bobbie, are you in there?'

Bobbie began squirming within her tiny prison, trying to tear the handcuffs apart. It was never going to succeed, but she gave it a good Irish try. The banging on the door was followed by a voice that made her cry. She heard her father shout "Bobbie" and she vowed there and then that she would never again go against a single syllable of his wishes. A tidal wave of relief flooded through her body. Tears blinded her. She almost choked, as she sobbed at the prospect of being freed.

The clank of a key in a door and then two voices, one her father's, grew louder.

'Open that one, I'll take this one,' she heard her father say.

Bobbie could barely breathe now; such was her impatience to be with her father. Within moments the casket opened. Light and air flooded inside bathing her skin. Temporarily blinded, she could only see a blurry figure looming over her.

'She's here,' said Barnes to Flynn.

Flynn spun around. The sarcophagus he'd opened was empty. All at once, the heavy weight that seemed to be constricting him lifted. He'd borne it too long. In one bound, he was over to where Barnes was standing. He looked in and saw his daughter bound with a gag digging into her mouth.

'Bobbie,' he cried and there were tears in his eyes. He crouched over her. With trembling hands and a heart that was about to explode, he attempted to pull the gag from her mouth.

Suddenly he collapsed on top of Bobbie. A swift and calculated blow by Larry Barnes struck the unsuspecting detective, sending him spiralling into the depths of unconsciousness like a stone thrown down a deep well. As Flynn crumpled over the sarcophagus, the world around him dissolved into a kaleidoscope of shadows, the echoes of his futile struggle fading into the ether.

Bobbie saw the blurred figure of the security guard smash the back of his father's head with a metallic object. She tried to scream, but her father hadn't been able to remove the gag in time. Bobbie strained once more with the handcuffs but, seconds later, she saw her father pulled roughly away and once more the lid of the coffin shut, plunging her and her hopes into darkness.

A torrent of emotions surged forth, mingling anguish with resignation, in a bitter symphony of desolation. She knew, with heart-breaking clarity, that it was no longer just her, but also her father who faced great danger. For her father would know who had attacked him.

They would have no choice.

They would have to kill him.

Larry Barnes tied a gag in Flynn's mouth and then bound his hands behind his back, as best he could, with a leather strap that was used to keep boxes in place. He was mouthing curses as he did so. Like Bobbie, he knew that a line had been crossed. Flynn would be able to name him as a conspirator in the robbery that was taking place. He would also become the number one suspect in the investigation to find Coletti's killer. In summary, he was in it up to his neck.

And he was angry.

The robbery was becoming a giant mess. The boss had said things would be complicated, but this was ridiculous. It was one thing to misdirect the police with a murder and the theft of the hippo, but they hadn't counted on the presence of a police inspector of all things, and his daughter visiting the gallery. It was a mess.

What would have to happen now was clear to Barnes. Flynn would have to be killed, probably his daughter too. She must have seen him club her father senseless and then yank him away from the casket. How could she not have seen him? If not there, then in the gallery when the lights went out.

He swore out loud and smacked the side of the storeroom. Of course, things like this never run smoothly, the boss had said as much. Yet Barnes could not escape the feeling that he was now the patsy. First Coletti and now him. The plan may not have set out that way, but this was now the reality. Killing a cop was something different, though. Coletti had it coming. He was an idiot. They nearly had to form a queue to do away with him. A cop, though?

His forehead was bathed in perspiration. He had to find the boss and let him know. He wouldn't be happy. They had been planning this for six months now. No, he wouldn't be happy at all.

He closed the door of the storeroom behind him and headed over to the office, to put the keys back. His mind was spinning with what might happen. It was meant to be complicated. That had always been understood. The success of the robbery depended on just this. Yet, both he and Coletti had always questioned why they needed to make it quite so intricate. It was asking for problems. And now the problems had come in droves.

The two Flynns had to die, that was clear. He'd have done it himself there and then, but best to check, first. As he was about to leave the basement area, the door opened.

Barnes looked at the new arrival and said, 'It's you. Good, I was just coming to find you. We have a problem. Flynn found his daughter.'

'Where is he now?' asked the new arrival.

'With her,' replied Barnes. His voice could not hide the anxiety he was feeling. 'Look, this is a mess. They'll be coming here any second, to start loading the paintings.'

'Don't worry about that. You just do your job.'

'They'll know it's me,' pointed out Barnes.

'Don't worry about that. When this is over and we've made our money, you'll be in Brazil or Mexico or Cuba. Just one more hour and we're free.'

Barnes nodded unhappily. This would be the longest hour of his life.

20

Duveen Gallery 5th Avenue and 56th Street, New York: April 1912

'Ah Morgan,' said Joseph Duveen, to his secretary. 'There you are. Sit down here old man while we practice.'

This was not the first time his lordship had made such a request. It did not make it any less of an imposition. He was no actor. Even at school, he had avoided their productions, where possible. A crowd scene was about the extent of his experience in the amateur dramatic world and now his lordship wanted to play the part of an American multi-millionaire who he wanted to interest in a painting.

Morgan looked at the two brothers before him. They were quite a contrast. Joseph, the eldest, was charismatic, a born snake oil salesman dressed in the clothes of a nobility from which he had not hailed. He navigated the social intricacies with the grace of a seasoned courtier, like a duck diving into a pristine pond. Almost single-handedly he had channelled the wealth of American elite into a frenzy of art collecting where the Gettys, the JP Morgans, the Fricks, the Mellons and the Altmans, were competing to buy the great treasures of European art. Morgan worshipped the man, as impossible as he could be.

Henry was a contrast. Easy-going, less of a salesman, but no less important in maintaining relationships with these prickly, narcissistic rich men. From time to time, it was necessary to dragoon Henry into the sales side of the equation, when Joseph felt that the potential buyer would not be so amenable to his more direct approach.

'So, Morgan, you'll be our man,' said Joseph.

'Who am I?' asked Morgan.

'Altman, haven't you been listening? You are old, single and make Ebenezer Scrooge seem like the very definition of philanthropy.'

'Mr Altman,' repeated Morgan who always spoke of Duveen's clients with respect. 'Which painting, may I ask?'

'The portrait. The Rembrandt,' snapped Joseph, keen to get on with the sales pitch he wanted Henry to memorise.

Morgan nodded, ready to do his bit, as always. Sometimes he wondered if his main qualification for being employed by the great man was the fact his surname was the same as the banker and Joseph just liked the sound of giving him orders. The thought rarely stayed long as he felt that he was an important part of the operation.

'Right-ho,' said Joseph. 'Now, you've just come in and sat down. Henry, listen to this. You know what Altman is like. No small talk. Straight to business. You'll say, "Benjamin, I've just sold two Rembrandts to Widener." What do you say to that?'

Silence followed this. The two Duveens looked at Morgan expectantly. Realising this was his cue, Morgan spoke in what he believed would be a reasonable representation of the old miser's likely response.

'Why should I care what Widener does?'

Joseph Duveen's eyes widened, 'Steady on old chap. That's a little bit too close to the bone.'

'Sorry, sir.'

'Anyway, Henry, this is where you play your ace card. He likes you. You can be honest with him. Say something like, "Benjamin, neither of us are young. We won't be here in twenty, thirty years' time. What is your legacy? The shops, of course. But what about your art collection? When you bequeath it, you'll want to have some big hitters in there. The crockery is all very well, but we don't eat crockery, we eat meat. Your collection has no meat. Yes, you have a Rembrandt or three, but you need to add to this collection its final jewel. You need to acquire one of his self-portraits.'

Morgan and Henry looked on, sceptically, at this impassioned plea. While essentially true, it was perhaps a little too much of a stretch to compare Renaissance masters or a Rembrandt to meat and potatoes.

'Trust me, appeal to his patriotism, his desire to leave a legacy, that future generations will thank him for, when he bequeaths this wonderful collection to the country,' said Joseph, 'You'll have your man. It always works.'

21

Something had been bugging Violet, as she and the patrolman, Mulcahy, were driving back to the orphanage. It had to be important, reasoned Violet, otherwise it wouldn't be so irritating. For the first ten minutes of the journey, she was silent. Mulcahy did not know Violet well but, as the father of three teenage girls, he did know eleven-years-old females were not naturally so quiet, even with cops.

Unusually for a policeman, Mulcahy had allowed Violet to sit with him at the front of the car. His reasoning was that she was not under arrest. They rode along in silence and then Mulcahy decided enough was enough.

'You're quiet,' he said in a thick Bronx accent.

Violet was still feeling overwhelmed with worry, but she did manage a sideways glance and a half smile.

'I'm worried,' she admitted. 'They'll find Bobbie, won't they?'

Mulcahy smiled sympathetically at the child and replied, 'Little lady, I've known Inspector Flynn longer than either of us cares to remember and I can tell you that he will move heaven and earth to find Red. As soon as I drop you off, I'll head straight back and help them.'

Violet smiled at this, but could feel the tears stinging her eyes, once more. She turned her attention to staring out of the window. In the distance she could see her home, the Roman Catholic Orphan Asylum, a large red brick building, that dominated the immediate skyline.

The cars and the people became a blur for Violet, as her tears fell. Still her mind turned over those moments before and after the lights went out. Try as she might she could not put things in the order that they had happened. It was exasperating. It felt as if she had held back something critical.

Mulcahy turned into the grounds of the orphanage and drove up to the front entrance. The arrival of a police car was rather uncommon, at the best of times and inevitably resulted in every child, who had access to a window, wanting to see what would emerge from the car.

That it was Violet was no surprise. More concerning was that she was visibly distressed as she exited the car. They watched the policeman take her hand and lead her up to the entrance.

Sister Assumpta had heard the commotion and was soon at the entrance to greet the little girl that she had taken to so much. The distress in the child broke her heart, but the reason for it worried her.

Where was Bobbie and her father?

Violet broke free from Mulcahy and ran to the elderly nun and buried her head in the navy habit.

'My child, what's wrong,' asked Sister Assumpta. She addressed Violet, but she was looking with a frown at Mulcahy.

A word about elderly Catholic nuns is appropriate at this juncture. That word is fearsome. Despite their deserved reputation for having a deep Christian faith and piety, there were some, in Mulcahy's experience, who had a predisposition towards violence that would made them a terrifying presence in Sing Sing, never mind at a school.

One look from the nun was enough to send Mulcahy's innards quaking and the memory of several hundred clips around the ear, for misbehaviour, returned to him, even though they had occurred decades previously. His hand went up. This was partly a request to speak and partly a self defence mechanism in case the nun decided to lash out with a left jab.

'It's not what you think,' said Mulcahy, echoing what many men have said to women over the years, although rarely to angry nuns.

Thankfully, providence, in the form of an eleven-year-old child, stepped in at this point to save Mulcahy from either verbal or physical evisceration, either were possible given the look in Sister Assumpta's eyes.

'Bobbie's missing,' said Violet.

Sister Assumpta stared down at Violet and then looked at Mulcahy for further enlightenment as Violet was sobbing once more.

As quickly as possible, for he was keen to return to the museum, Mulcahy explained what had occurred. Violet occasionally interjected a point or two so that the matter was now cleared up to Sister Assumpta's satisfaction and Mulcahy's physical wellbeing.

Just as he was about to depart to the museum, Violet called him back.

'There's something I forgot to mention to Inspector Flynn and Detective Nolan. Can you tell them? I'm not sure how important it is.'

'Of course,' said Mulcahy, keeping one eye on Violet and one eye on the nun, just in case.

'It was after the lights went out. I heard the glass shatter. There was lots of shouting and screaming but I heard another noise. I don't know how to describe it. It was like something falling on the ground. A clang.'

'A person?' asked Mulcahy.

'No, it might have been a gun or something quite heavy. And then we were knocked over and then...'

Mulcahy nodded as the girl could not find the words to continue and describe when Bobbie was abducted.

'You were right to tell me,' he said in a kindly voice and then, with a nod to Sister Assumpta, he returned to the car.

Sister Assumpta knelt and put her two hands on the cheeks of Violet.

'Be strong my child. They'll find her.'

22

Detective Nolan and Dick Devenish, although neither would admit it, were a little less certain of this as they trooped back to the meeting room at five thirty empty-handed. Lewis was already there and one look from the grizzled patrolman told them that he had been no more successful. Nolan remained unsure about Lewis and had already decided that he might check the floor, with some other men that he knew he could trust.

'No sign of Miss Flynn?' asked Nolan.

'No,' replied Lewis, throwing his cap on the table in frustration.

'Where's Inspector Flynn and Barnes,' asked Nolan, surprised that the inspector was not with them.

'He was supposed to go to the conservation area and the basement,' reminded Lewis, although Nolan hardly needed reminding of this.

'Odd,' said Devenish, which was unusually succinct for him.

Nolan agreed. It was odd, but Flynn was a law unto himself and he was in the middle of a personal crisis. It was inevitable he would want to keep searching every last inch of the building. The reality hit Nolan just then. He was standing in a room with men, none of whom he trusted. Devenish and

Lewis had question marks over them and there were a couple of security staff by the door. All of them were looking at Nolan, expectantly.

'Aside from the administrative offices' asked Nolan, is there any part of the building that has not been searched?' wondered Nolan out loud. He turned to one of the security men who had accompanied Lewis. Nolan continued, 'For example, are there any outbuildings?'

The security guard shook his head without saying anything. Nolan felt growing frustration at their inability to make progress. The abduction had happened out in the open, albeit in a room that had been temporarily blacked out. It would have required a minimum of two men to carry out the robbery and the abduction. Once out of the room they would need to have hidden Bobbie quickly, as they could not have gone very far, without running into someone. In all likelihood, they would have taken the non-public route. They would have taken the stairs, that led from the room where the robbery had taken place.

'We'll head back to the Egyptian gallery,' announced Nolan. 'I want to retrace the route the robbers might have taken.'

Just as he said the this, there was a brief knock at the door. Edward Robinson appeared with the security chief, Sampson. Any hope on his face was extinguished, immediately, by the grave faces and the atmosphere in the room.

'No sigh of Bobbie?' he asked, in a voice already betraying his anxiety.

'I'm afraid not,' replied Devenish.

'And Flynn? Any news of how he's getting on?' asked Robinson.

Nolan groaned inwardly at this and replied, 'He was down in the basement storage area.'

Robinson frowned at this, 'Really? I was just down there myself a few minutes ago. The truck to take the paintings to the liner is being loaded.'

'And you didn't see him?' asked Nolan, surprised.

Robinson frowned and replied, 'No. Strange. I would have thought someone would have said that he was nearby.'

This didn't feel right. Nolan was growing more alarmed now but tried to remain outwardly composed. His suspicions of Barnes, the man who had accompanied his boss, were mounting. But then this seemed to apply to all the security team. Sampson was an enigma. And, if he was an enigma, he was also someone that Nolan sensed you did not cross.

Just as they were about to head up to the Egyptian gallery, there was a knock at the door. It was Mulcahy having returned from delivering Violet back to the orphanage. Nolan was relieved to see him. This was someone he knew he could trust. The patrolman entered the room and quickly scanned for his old friend Flynn. One look at the grave faces and he said, almost fearfully, 'What's happened?' He'd known Bobbie since she was a child. The atmosphere he encountered in the room led him to fear the worst.

'Come with us, Mulcahy,' said Nolan, quickly. 'We may have another problem on our hands. The inspector is missing. I want to retrace the route the robbers might have taken.'

'I'll have to leave you, Detective Nolan,' said Robinson. 'But I may see you in the basement. I'll need Sampson to come with me to oversee the paintings being loaded onto the truck.'

'I understand,' replied Nolan.

They separated at this point with Nolan leading Devenish, Lewis and Mulcahy up the stairs to the Egyptian Gallery where the robbery had taken place, while the two museum men went down to the storage area.

As they climbed the stairs Devenish, who had been silent for too long, spoke up.

'Can we trust that man Sampson? I gather he has a rather interesting past; I don't know if you are aware?'

Nolan turned to Devenish in surprise. How did he know this?

'In answer to the question you want to ask me; Robinson asked me to investigate the background of Sampson. You're obviously aware of what he did.'

'I am,' said Nolan. 'I suppose it's a surprise that he was still able to get this job.'

'Ah, Detective Nolan, perhaps you should have dug a little bit more.'

'How do you mean?' quizzed Nolan.

'Mr Sampson may have had an unfortunate end to his police career, but prior to that he was an exemplary member of the police department, with many citations.'

'It doesn't mean that a spell in the can hasn't turned him,' pointed out Nolan.

'I don't disagree,' said Devenish. 'This has all the hallmarks of an inside job. No one is better placed to have organised it than our former policeman. I would keep an eye on him if I were you.'

Nolan fully intended doing so, and not just on Sampson either. They trooped along, in silence, until they reached the gallery. By the time they had arrived, many of the people who had been in the room had now departed, having given statements.

Captain Frank O'Riordan was in the room now, having been called away from his usual Sunday afternoon at home. He did not look happy about this. That said, any good humour in this man had long since taken a holiday. He spun around when notified of Nolan's arrival, almost causing the hat, perched precariously on the back of his head, to fall off.

The sight of Nolan returning did little to improve his mood. His cigar drooped from his mouth in weary resignation of what lay ahead.

'So, no sign of Flynn's daughter, I take it?' barked O'Riordan, without bothering to remove his cigar.

'No,' replied Nolan.

'Meddling women. This is what happens,' snarled O'Riordan unsympathetically.

Nolan controlled the temptation to smack the captain and said tersely, 'Has the inspector been here?'

This brought a frown from O'Riordan. He said, 'Don't tell me he's missing too.'

'We're not sure at the moment, sir,' replied Nolan.

'There's no sign of the inspector or his daughter,' admitted Nolan.

'Great,' said O'Riordan, clearly not meaning this. Then he looked at Devenish and grimaced.

Devenish noted this and said with relish, 'Ah Captain O'Riordan, how lovely to see you too. I'm sure you'll have this cleared up in no time,' mocked Devenish.

'Without your help,' snapped O'Riordan.

'I don't doubt it, Captain O'Riordan. You are a veritable one-man crime-fighting machine. But if it's all the same to you,

I think that I shall stick around anyway. Who knows what I may learn from a keen-eyed cop like yourself? I daresay you already have a few theories about the robbery and the kidnapping?'

Nothing on O'Riordan's face suggested he had so much as one idea. Silence followed this, as O'Riordan looked away from the source of the scorn. In fact, he seemed at a loss on what to do next. Most of the witnesses had been questioned and had departed. Flynn was meant to be here too, and now he was possibly missing-in-action. The whole thing was spiralling into one disarray that was playing havoc with his day off.

Nolan, who for many reasons, had no time for the captain, filled the vacuum that had taken over the large room.

'I was going to take Lewis and Mulcahy to continue the search for Miss Flynn and, perhaps, the inspector.'

O'Riordan nodded at this and semi-waved them away. He watched them leave the room, then he glanced sharply at Devenish. The private investigator smiled, bowed slightly and said, in a self-effacing manner that fooled no one, 'May I speak to some of the remaining witnesses, and to your men who have been questioning the others? I do have a modest knack for seeing things that others have not.'

'I wish you could modestly see the exit and clear the hell out of here,' scowled O'Riordan.

This was about the first time the captain had said something that Nolan concurred with. Just as he was about to take his leave, Mulcahy stepped forward and cleared his throat.

'There's one thing I think you should know,' said the patrolman. All eyes turned on him. He was unused to having an audience like this. 'It's about the kid. Violet.'

'Go on,' snapped O'Riordan, irritably.

'She said she heard a sound right after the glass was shattered. She'd forgotten to mention it.'

'What was this sound?' asked O'Riordan sarcastically. It was clear he had little or no interest in the answer.

Mulcahy's eyes narrowed a little and he looked like he was a few seconds away from giving the captain a few choice words. Instead, common sense prevailed. He took a deep breath, that was audible enough to be interpreted by everyone, O'Riordan included, as a Herculean effort on Mulcahy's part not to separate the captain's noggin from the rest of his body. 'Well, it was a thud sound. Like something hard falling on the ground. Not a body. It was like an object,' he added.

It took a few seconds for everyone to process this and then O'Riordan dismissed it out of hand.

'It can't have been the damn hippo. It would have broken into pieces.'

'A thud?' asked Devenish, who was more interested in what Violet had said. 'Did she describe the sound in any more detail?'

'Thud schmud,' replied O'Riordan supportively.

'I'm interested Captain O'Riordan,' interjected Devenish. 'Were those her words?'

'She said it was like a clang,' answered Mulcahy, relieved that someone was taking it seriously.

Devenish nodded his head to this and asked, 'Nothing else?'

'No. Just a clang. Definitely not a body.'

Devenish pondered this for a few moments. He shut his eyes as if trying to place himself in the room at the time of the robbery. He went through the order of the events as he'd heard them described by several witnesses and now by Violet.

A smile broke out on Devenish's face.

'Of course,' he exclaimed excitedly which made O'Riordan scowl even more. 'Of course.'

23

A similar thought regarding the sounds she'd heard crossed the mind of Bobbie earlier, but this had been wiped from her mind following the terrifying moment when she had seen her father assaulted from behind. It had been twenty minutes since she'd seen her father and then seen him disappear.

He'd been knocked unconscious, that much was clear. She'd seen him being pulled from her casket and then the lid had closed. Then she had heard something else that definitely sounded like a casket being opened and closed followed by the door of the storage room being locked.

Time seemed to stretch endlessly; it usually does when one is in despair. The darkness of the coffin enveloped her, along with a mood of hopelessness. She had long since accepted that struggling against her bonds was only likely to burn up valuable oxygen inside the casket.

The air inside the tiny space was once thicker and staler. Her oxygen supply was beginning to dwindle, once more. Each breath she took reminded her that the clock was ticking down, until the point at which it would run out. If her father was in the other sarcophagus, and she believed he was, then he was in similar peril.

The lack of fresh oxygen, over the last hour and a half, was beginning to tell. Her mind was finding it difficult to concentrate on one thing. Her head thumping was not ever likely to help her focus. She was pretty sure she had fallen unconscious. Images floated through her mind. Her father, once more. Violet.

The robbery.

She saw the lights going out. Then she saw the moments before this had happened. She saw it with perfect clarity. She saw the man who had approached her from behind.

The man she'd seen in the gallery just before the lights went out was the same man who had hit her father. It was Larry Barnes, the security guard.

Her eyes shot open and she wanted to scream. The blurred figure she had seen loom over her father before striking him. Larry Barnes. She was sure of it.

And then, she heard voices outside her storage unit. They were dim. Despite this she could hear Edward Robinson. She was sure it was him. Then another voice and then another. The final one she knew also.

Detective Nolan.

She was alive. Yet, with this came the gnawing sense of impotence, as she squirmed in her tiny prison. Surely, he must have been aware that she was missing. Surely, he would be aware that her father, too, was missing.

It was impossible to hear what they were saying, despite how much she strained to listen. She found herself cursing both Robinson and Nolan as, unlike most men, they did not feel the need to speak in a loud voice.

She waited for the door to open.

And then she heard shouting.

24

Benjamin Altman's 5th Avenue townhouse, New York: November 1912

The drawing room of Benjamin Altman's 5th Avenue townhouse presented a welcome contrast to the rest of the house, in that it was warm. The fire was, by any standards, roaring. It crackled and spat and hissed in a manner that was at odds with the chilly nature of the rest of the house. The room was dark, lit only by the fire, but this was not altogether a bad thing thought Edward Robinson. Above the fireplace hung the picture that he'd come to view. The one that would, one day, adorn the walls of the Metropolitan Museum thanks to the largesse of the man who was sitting across from him and, particularly, the man who was not here, Lord Joseph Duveen.

It was a delicate subject, however. Rather like a prince, he had to wait for the death of the king before what he craved could become his. Robinson was used to dealing with men such as Altman. In his own way he was their equal. A man who had risen to the summit of Mount Olympus in his chosen profession. There was a disparity in wealth, but Robinson came from a class that had enjoyed affluence long before any of these new men had earned their fortune.

Robinson was standing before the Rembrandt and gazed, in awe, at the portrait. A self-portrait by the great man. The black hat was tipped at an angle which made Robinson smile. There was life in the old dog even then, despite all the tragedy and the money troubles.

'Do you like it?' barked Altman before his voice gave way to wracking coughs. He was old. Dying. Shrinking physically but his mind would never submit to the frailty of age.

'Of course,' replied Robinson, unable to tear his eyes away from those of the artist, depicted in the picture.

'Why?' asked Altman. He seemed curious.

Robinson glanced down at the seated man. Altman was a man in his seventies. He looked it and more. He had a tartan rug over his knees. His body shook with the cough that Robinson suspected might kill him.

'I scarcely know where to begin, Mr Altman. It's beautiful, even if Rembrandt, himself, is not. The beauty of the work lies deeper. It's in the eyes of this man; it's in the brushwork; it's in the very conception of painting yourself throughout your life without any attempt to hide from the worries you've had, the dreams that have been shattered, the hard, daily slog of living when sometimes you just want to stop and shout, "Enough." It's so many things and this wonderful man, this genius, captures it all for us to see and experience centuries later. This is truth Mr Altman. It's undistorted truth. How often do you encounter that, Mr Altman?'

'Not often,' snapped Altman, before breaking out, once more, into a cough that seemed to choke his windpipe. He turned dangerously red.

Robinson had to steel himself from flinching at the sight of the dying man.

'May I ask who your doctor is? I have a very good man...'

Altman interrupted him with a wave of the hand.

'They're all quacks. They'd steal the shirt off your back and give you some snake oil. It's nothing.'

This was deluded, but Robinson refrained from saying so. Instead, he shifted the conversation to the subject that he had come to discuss.

'Mr Altman, I don't know if you are aware, but many of our supporters often experience great joy in seeing their own painting hanging on the walls of the museum. Have you considered perhaps loaning us this painting so that you, too, could see it along with the many devotees of this artist?'

Altman studied Robinson closely. Then he growled, *'Go on.'*

'We would, of course, notify the press of the loan. I imagine this is something that might reflect well, not just on you, but on your department stores. We could have an evening at the museum, where we invite many of the city's notables and a few friendly members of the press. I'm sure that it would be a tremendous success. This, after all, is an extraordinary painting. Alongside your other Rembrandts it would make the exhibition an outstanding success.'

Whether Benjamin Altman knew he was dying or not, even he could not tell. He had overcome so much adversity already, in his seventy-two years, what was another cold?

'All of the Rembrandts, you say?'

'Yes, sir. It would be quite something to see them in one room. The Vermeer too and the Memlings. Your Dutch collection is probably the foremost in the world still in private hands. Your collection is probably close to priceless. I think I am not exaggerating if I say it would be a sensation.'

Altman nodded. His eyes drooped a little and, for a sickening moment, Robinson worried he might expire there and then. After a few moments his eyes shot open. He said one word. It was a word he'd used often in his dealmaking over the years.

'Done.'

25

Nolan arrived in the basement area, to find a few of the men and women he'd met earlier. Aside from Robinson and Sampson, there were three of the people from the art department, head curator, Professor Pearson and the two conservators, Roscoe Meredith and Sarah Mason. They were watching as boxed up paintings were loaded onto a van. By the van was a tall, fair-haired man who was speaking heavily accented English.

Robinson went over to Nolan as soon as he, Mulcahy and Lewis appeared in the basement. There was a look of concern on his face.

'Detective Nolan,' said Robinson. 'Is there any sign yet of Bobbie, or Flynn for that matter.'

'Not yet,' admitted Nolan. We've come to look in these storage units, I hope you don't mind.'

'Of course not. Let me introduce you to Professor Wouters first and then I'll let you go.'

Robinson called the tall Dutchman over. He was around forty years of age and dressed in a sober suit. He sported a beard which probably aged him a little but gave him a certain gravitas.

'Professor Wouters, may I introduce Detective Nolan. He is one of the men from the New York Police Department who is investigating the robbery.'

The two men shook hands. He had a firm grip and looked Nolan in the eye. His face was serious and there did not seem to be many laugh lines around his eyes.

'I wish you luck Detective Nolan. This artefact is of great value and much loved, I gather.'

Nolan had no idea but decided to nod politely at this comment. He said something about doing their best which, even to his ears, sounded trite and inadequate. He was desperate to get away and search the storerooms and perhaps this was evident in his eyes.

Robinson smiled and said in a solemn voice, 'We won't detain you any longer.'

Nolan turned away to join Mulcahy and Lewis. Just as he did so, a patrolman came bursting in, and he shouted over to the men before him, 'Nolan, Mulcahy, Lewis, Captain O'Riordan wants you upstairs, pronto. Mr Robinson, you may want to come too.'

Despite being on the wrong side of sixty, Nolan, the patrolmen and Sampson had difficulty in keeping up with the Museum Director. There was something in the tone of the new arrival's voice, that gave him hope that good news awaited him upstairs.

The men burst through the door of the gallery, the same side door that, just over an hour and a half earlier, had been the door through which Bobbie had been removed from the Egyptian room. They were greeted by an uncommon sight.

Captain O'Riordan was holding a small, blue ceramic hippo. His face had a decidedly thunderous aspect, somewhat at odds to the news he had to communicate. To Nolan, it looked as if he was experiencing the worst moment of his life. The reason for this was not hard to guess if the beaming countenance of the man beside him, Dick Devenish, was anything to go by. O'Riordan's mood was not helped by the first delighted comment from Robinson.

'You found it!' exclaimed Robinson, barely able to contain his delight

O'Riordan had clearly not found it and being congratulated for this was only rubbing salt into the wound. Still, it was probably worth giving up his day off for this. By the time he wrote his report on the finding he would be able to diminish the role of Devenish and add the successful outcome to enhance his own status. A year from now, no one would remember what had happened, and he would have it on his record that the case was closed successfully.

He began to feel better about the situation, even if it did gall him that it was Devenish, of all people, who had found the solution. By the look on his face, he was about to embark on his lap of honour with the new arrivals. In any other circumstance he would have put a speedy stop to any self-aggrandising summary from the arrogant fat head, but as Robinson was there and keen to hear what had happened, he had to break the habit of a lifetime and remain silent.

'No, this isn't the real one. It came from the museum shop. I just wanted to see what it looked like,' said O'Riordan glumly.

'So, we don't have the hippo?' asked Robinson, tersely.

'We do,' announced Devenish. With a sly glance towards O'Riordan, he added, 'I know where the artefact is hidden.' This angered the policeman, as it was intended to. Fully aware of O'Riordan's growing impatience, Devenish continued remorselessly, 'Doubtless you would like to know how the solution came to me.'

Probably only Robinson and Devenish, himself, were interested in hearing this. Nolan was feeling exasperation, but for entirely different reasons. He wanted to get back down to the storage area and continue the search. There was no question in his mind now, something *had* happened to the inspector.

'It was really quite straightforward when you think about it. Rather ingenious too and, I think, Robinson, it suggests a bigger problem for you which I will come to,' began Devenish.

He paused to make sure, like a teacher in a classroom, that he had everyone's attention, then he continued, 'The missing clue was provided by the waif. Unlike our noble captain here, I was not prepared to disregard a child's memory of what had happened. As late in the day as it may have been, it was the critical point in the discovery of dear old William.'

'What?' exclaimed Robinson. 'Which child?'

'Violet, the young lady that accompanied Miss Flynn and her father. They were eyewitnesses, in a manner of speaking. Or should I say in this case, earwitnesses.'

This brought a smile from Devenish which widened when he saw that everyone was appalled by the pun. 'Well, it amused me anyway,' he added shamelessly.

Nolan was almost hopping from one foot to another, such was his impatience for the private investigator to get to the point.

'This highly alert young lady picked up on a clue, immediately disregarded of course by New York's finest because the source was considered untrustworthy. Only I realised the importance of what she had said.'

'What had she said?' asked Nolan, in a voice that he hoped conveyed the boredom that was setting in with this charade.

Devenish eyed Nolan and saw the anger in his eyes. Oddly, his brief time with the young detective had proved enough for him have judged him a bit better than the average cop. The evident impatience was clearly borne from a desire to continue with the search. It dawned on Devenish that the reveal would not have the effect he had hoped.

'It was pitch black. Violet remembered hearing a thud immediately after the glass shattered. The lights were out of course. One of the men, for there were two, abducted Miss Flynn while his confederate snatched William. Except that he didn't. William never left the room.'

Devenish stepped forward towards the plinth, crunching over the broken glass. He put his hand on top of the plinth and pressed downwards. His hand and part of his arm disappeared, before reappearing a moment later, clutching the ceramic blue hippo.

'Here he is, safe and sound,' said Devenish, with a wide grin. He glanced towards Nolan as if seeking an apology.

To his surprise he received one. It was only a nod, barely noticeable. Yet, it meant something to the private investigator. He stepped forward and handed William to Robinson.

Then he returned his gaze to Nolan.

'I gather we still have an inspector and his beautiful daughter to find. Well, let's go. No point in wasting any more time here.'

26

A subject that may one day have the great philosophers, from Socrates to Bertrand Russell, bunching up to allow space for a new candidate, is an explanation of why women reserve their greatest ire for those men they profess to love.

It must be said that Bobbie's feelings towards Detective Nolan in the run up to her incarceration in the sarcophagus were, even by the elevated standards of the opposite camp, pretty complicated. Falling for someone who you, firmly, believe to be in the employ of mobsters, is a tricky business, at the best of times. When your father is a cop, of unimpeachable integrity, the situation gets worse.

Even if she believed that said young man was flexible of principle, the sound of his voice nearby, as she lay incarcerated in the sarcophagus, provoked feelings in her that she had been resolute in resisting in recent weeks.

Then she heard the shouting and, what to her mind, sounded like the potential hero of the hour exiting the stage, just as he was about to rescue this particular damsel.

At first Bobbie was not sure if the sound of shouting had heralded the departure of the potential rescuers. She was prepared to wait, for what else could she do? One minute passed and then two. No door burst open; no lid being lifted.

Nothing. The search, as far as she could tell, had been abandoned before it had even begun.

The realisation that she was, once more, alone was greeted in the only manner that was appropriate in such circumstances...

Fury.

Especially as the reason for her continued confinement could be laid at the door of one, fat-headed man, Nolan.

All thought of conserving oxygen were abandoned. If she could have howled in frustration at men generally, and Nolan specifically, she would have. However, the gag denied her that right. Instead, her body convulsed and she kicked and wriggled with a violence borne of anger and fear. For her thoughts were still very much focussed on the fate of her father.

The sheer force of her movements provoked a surprising realisation. The casket had rocked. She stopped for a moment to take that thought in. If the sarcophagus was on the ground, then her ability to make it rock would have been limited. But it had moved. This suggested to her that it was on a table and that her movements had shifted the casket's position.

One thing was clear to her. The heat and stuffiness of her confinement was overwhelming. She had to assume that her father was similarly imprisoned. The alternative did not bear thinking about.

She began to twist and turn as violently as she could. There was definite movement. She could sense it. She could hear it. She rocked herself back and forth as forcefully as her cramped confines would permit.

The sarcophagus was moving.

Bobbie's movement became almost frenzied. The ferocity with which she slammed herself from side to side bordered on madness, yet she could feel the casket shift until...

It fell.

It fell with an almighty clatter to the ground. Several thousand years of antiquity splintered. The lid opened, albeit with her face down on the ground. More importantly, fresh air flooded into the space.

Bobbie waited a minute to listen to the sounds outside. She could hear voices a little bit more clearly now. They did not seem to have heard her. This was, possibly, due to the hammering of nails outside, that echoed around the large storage area like a thousand cannons in the middle of a relentless siege.

This provoked a few words in Bobbie's mind that were unlikely to grace any obituary she would write, anytime soon. She breathed in deeply to recover her strength and endeavour to make one last effort to free herself. She rolled herself over so that her back was on the ground. Next, she hunched her knees as she tried to raise the sarcophagus up high enough from the ground to allow her to roll free.

It took a couple of attempts, but finally she managed to extricate herself from the coffin. It took a moment to adjust her eyes to the dim light in the storeroom. Then she took stock of where she was. On one side, was the damaged sarcophagus. Bobbie did feel a stab of guilt at what her escape had wrought. It was momentary. True responsibility for this crime lay elsewhere.

Next, she looked around her and saw that the room was full of wooden crates. However, her heartbeat, already somewhat raised, raced faster, as she saw another sarcophagus at the far end of the room. There were tears in her eyes once more. She was so close. For the next few moments, she concentrated on her breathing. The situation was still challenging. Her hands were cuffed behind her back. Her ankles were bound with some strapping. The first thing she needed to do was move her hands to the front of her body. This would allow her to remove the gag and strapping. Moving her hands to the front of her body required a feat of gymnastics, that would have been beyond many. Thankfully, Bobbie was very slender. This would make the task easier.

She scrunched her body into a foetal position and slowly manoeuvred her hands around the soles of her feet, probably tearing half a dozen sinews, in the painful process. But soon, she had her hands back in the right hemisphere. The gag was off in an instant quickly followed by the strapping around her ankles.

Her hair was matted with perspiration, her heart was racing, like a quarter horse down the home straight, and her breathing came in gasps, but she was free. She climbed awkwardly to her feet and, without so much as a quick dusting down, she flew over to the other sarcophagus. The tension in her chest was almost painful, as she wrenched open the lid.

Her father lay inside, eyes closed, dried blood on the side of his face. The gag in his mouth was, paradoxically, a good sign. He was also handcuffed, but there was little chance that her father could pull of the feat of flexibility that Bobbie had. She pulled the gag away from his mouth and checked for signs that he was breathing.

He was. The pulse was not strong, but it was sufficient to reassure Bobbie that the worst her father might suffer was a sore head for a day or two. As his usual manner suggested that he had this anyway, Bobbie doubted she would notice much difference in him.

It was time to get help.

Just as this thought occurred to her, she heard voices outside. She stifled the instinct to shout. There was a chance that the help she received would merely be a return to a cramped space with a gag and handcuffs. Or worse. The memory of her abduction was too fresh. No, she would have to check on whether the men outside were to be trusted.

With a glance of apology to her father, Bobbie kicked off her shoes and padded over to the door. Pressing her ear against the metal wall, she strained to listen in on what was being said. The conversation was difficult to hear with the banging that was going on. The men appeared to be discussing progress on packing the paintings into their crates. One man shouted on several occasions for the other men to take greater care.

Bobbie sifted through her memories of the day to make sense of what was happening outside. She recalled both Edward Robinson and Sarah Mason mentioning a loan, that had been organised to the Rijksmuseum in Amsterdam. She wondered if they were referring to that. A few moments later, she heard someone mention Rembrandt. This all but confirmed in her the suspicion that this was what was happening outside. This being the case, she thought there was hardly any point in being cautious.

Just as she was about to bang on the door, she heard some other voices. Two of them were very familiar. No, make that three. Once more she struggled to hear what was being said, but then the rattle of keys cut through the noise echoing around the basement.

They were finally searching the storerooms.

One by one she heard the doors opening. One by one she heard someone shout.

'They're not here.'

Tempted as she was to bang on the door and alert them to where she was, Bobbie decided to wait her turn.

The sound of voices grew louder. In fact, they were in the next storeroom but one. To give Nolan his due, his voice was very clear now. To Bobbie's ears, there was more than a trace of anxiety in his voice. Devenish, unusually, sounded serious also. He was clearly trying to placate the detective, who was urging greater speed.

A little bit late in the day, thought Bobbie. Where have you been for the last hour and a half, Detective Nolan? She had every intention of picking up this subject with him when the door opened. Which, by her calculations, was less than a minute away.

27

Boardroom, Metropolitan Museum of Art, New York: October 1921

Edward Robinson sat at the head of the table, a position he had occupied for almost twelve years. He was a reassuring sight, whether he was speaking or silent. His very presence conveyed stability, common sense and fairness. Not one of the board of directors had any doubts on this score. Robinson knew this and, when the occasion demanded, played on it. This was one such occasion. He sensed that this was one of those rare occasions that he may not have the majority on his side.

He decided against standing up. It might appear too threatening. Or pompous. This was not his way and never would be. He said, 'The final item on the agenda is the proposed loan, of some of the Altman collection, to the Rijksmuseum in Amsterdam. Now I know when I first raised this, some of you, understandably, expressed some concerns.'

He paused for a moment, to see the reaction to his acknowledgement that there were doubts. A few of the men in the room raised an eyebrow.

'There are several reasons that, I think, make this a good move for our museum to consider. Compared to an institution

such as the Rijksmuseum, we are young. We are still growing. We do not have the treasures on offer that such an institution has. Yet, I might add...'

'So why, in the name of Paul Henry, are we loaning some of our best pieces?' said a dissenting voice.

Robinson smiled at this, as it was not unanticipated.

'We need to send a message to our cousins across the Atlantic. For we want this loan, not just to be appreciated by Amsterdam, but by London, Florence, Berlin and Paris. We want them to see that we are one of them. We want them to see us as a trusted part of a larger entity. We must be willing to share our greatest treasures, in order to receive and display other great works of art, in return. And we are growing. Every year our collection expands and many of the great museums will have noted that our pockets are deep. Rather than have them resent this, let us engage now with them to build good relationships.'

'While we raid Europe of its antiquities, thanks to Duveen?' added the same voice.

The table broke out into polite chuckles at this but, it seemed to Robinson, that they were swinging behind him now.

'I would not quite go that far Robert, but if it helps you support this plan, then I might concede this is an unintended benefit and please don't minute that,' replied Robinson with a smile.

There was more laughter at this and it seemed as if the room was falling behind him.

'We have been fortunate that one of our team has developed a good relationship with the Head Curator of Art at the museum, Professor Wouters. I shall let him take you *through the plan regarding the loan, its duration and, most importantly, its safe and secure arrival in Amsterdam.'*

28

Protocol, good sense and, probably a desire for self-preservation, dictate that it is best for detectives not to grab a young woman and kiss her, when she has either just been rescued following a kidnap, is angry with you or, in this case, both.

This was certainly on Detective Nolan's mind when he opened the door of the storage unit to find himself face to face with a young woman, with whom he was having to accept, he harboured feelings for. Any thought of taking her in his arms and sweeping her off her feet, in the manner prescribed by countless novelists of a romantic ilk, was immediately ended, not so much by her bedraggled appearance, but with the glint in her eye that even a mere man, such as Nolan, could tell was anger. Quite why this was the case was something only the young woman knew, and it was not guaranteed that she would ever enlighten him.

She did.

'Where the hell have you been?' she shouted at the unfortunate detective. Dick Devenish, for once, was glad not to have been the man who opened the door. As Bobbie followed this inquiry with something a good deal less printable.

If Nolan had suspected that something had gone awry in his interaction with Bobbie recently, then he was under no illusions now. However, having faced the might of the Kaiser's army only a few years before and survived relatively unscathed, he was not without some resources of his own, such as courage, duty and, in this case, a sense of outrage at the manifest unfairness of the indictments levelled against him.

'I've spent the last hour and a half looking for you and then your father.'

Her father.

'He needs a doctor,' said Bobbie, finally feeling both her anger and her emotions break. She turned to the sarcophagus at the back of the storeroom.

Nolan brushed past her and ran to the casket. Meanwhile, Devenish who had enjoyed the skirmish more than any man had a right to, murmured to Bobbie, 'He's been all over the museum looking for you, Red. You were a little unfair there.'

Tears of anger, relief and fear welled up inside Bobbie, but she refused to let them fall. Devenish could see the upset and the fear, in her eyes. He took her in his arms and gave her the hug that was so palpably needed at that moment.

Nolan turned around to see Bobbie being comforted by Devenish. This was not important at that moment. The inspector was unconscious and had received a very bad blow.

'Someone call for a doctor. We need an ambulance here immediately.'

Lewis, who was standing in the doorway, immediately offered to go. He turned and sprinted across to the security office where there was a telephone. He picked up the receiver and held the candlestick phone to his mouth.

There was no sound.

A security man popped his head through the door.

'It's not working, sir. The one upstairs should be working.'

Robinson appeared at this moment. There was a mixture of frustration and worry on his face.

'What's wrong?' he snapped. This was unusual, for the invariably unflappable museum head, but the events of the day were beginning to tell. As soon as he heard, he said, 'Come with me up to the office. We'll organise the very best help for Flynn.'

Lewis followed Robinson out of the security office. Devenish and Bobbie watched them go with a frown.

'I wonder what's going on there?' asked Devenish. Bobbie had no time to worry. She went over to where Nolan was sitting by her father.

The minute or two with Devenish had somewhat calmed Bobbie and she realised that her words to the detective might have been a little unfair. A feeling of remorse had taken up residence now, in her mind, and she fumbled around trying to find the right words, to express this regret to someone she believed to be acting against her father and the precinct. Finding the right balance can be damnably tricky.

'I'm sorry,' stuttered Bobbie. Tears were trickling down her cheek which was enough for Nolan to forgive her immediately, although the mystery of her change in behaviour towards him remained. Where once she had been, dare he hoped, flirtatious, she was now colder. Was this entirely the doing of her father? Possibly, but Bobbie had not struck him as the sort of girl to go meekly along with anyone's wishes, least of all her father's.

'What happened?' asked Nolan in a low voice, as if not wanting to wake the inspector. This, perhaps, was the obvious question to be addressed now, while they waited for medical help to arrive.

'It was Barnes, the security guard. He stole the hippo. He put me in the sarcophagus. I'm sure of it.'

Nolan looked away sharply and in anger.

'What's wrong?' asked Bobbie alarmed. 'Where's Violet?'

Nolan shook his head and replied, 'Violet's safe. Mulcahy took her back to the orphanage. We need to call them to let her know you're okay. She was worried sick about you.'

'Thank goodness she's safe. But why were you so angry about Barnes?'

'He was with your father. I think he's the one who did this to him. They were together when we went searching for you.'

'Where is he now?' asked Bobbie, her eyes wide with the horror of what had happened to her unsuspecting father.

'He's nowhere to be found. It's like he disappeared into thin air.'

'What about the theft?'

Nolan held his hand up and gestured towards Devenish, who was on his way over towards them.

'Lover boy found it. Thanks to Violet, I might add.'

Bobbie was too anxious to take in all what Nolan had said at that moment. She stared down at her father and found her throat tighten with the tension she was feeling. It was the worst she could remember feeling, since the death of her mother. The thumping headache was almost a welcome distraction, from the anxious knot in her stomach.

Devenish joined Bobbie and Nolan by the sarcophagus. He looked in and saw the inspector. His face was, for once, sombre.

'How is he?'

Bobbie shook her head but could say nothing.

'He's alive,' said Nolan. 'Someone went to get help?'

'Yes,' replied Devenish. He put a consoling hand on Bobbie's shoulder and said soothingly, 'Try not worry old thing. The softest part of him is his teeth.'

This, at least, brought a smile from Bobbie and she nodded. Then a thought struck her and she looked up at Devenish and asked, 'You found William?'

'Yes. Thanks to Violet.'

'Violet? Really? How?'

'She's really quite a remarkable young lady you know. If you are planning to adopt her then I, for one, would commend you. She described a sound that she'd heard immediately after the glass shattered. No one else heard it. Only her. It was all the clue I needed to solve the mystery.'

The last comment came with a certain bout of the verve that Devenish could not keep restrained for long. Nolan glanced at him with a sardonic look that Bobbie noticed. It might have made her smile in any other circumstance.

'Barnes did all of this? I'm not sure I buy that,' said Bobbie, clearly surprised by the scale of what was happening.

'Barnes the security guard?' asked Devenish, his moment of triumph punctured, somewhat, by the fact that although they had recovered the stolen object, they were no nearer finding the perpetrators.

Bobbie, continued almost to herself, 'He must have been working in league with others. He can't have planned and executed, all of this by himself.'

'True,' said Devenish. 'Which begs the question of course: who?'

'And why?' added Bobbie. 'They stole William, but not really. What's going on?'

Outside they heard the hammering of nails on crates containing treasures of Dutch art that were to be loaned back to the country in which they had been created.

'Where is that ambulance?' asked Bobbie in frustration. Then she rubbed her pounding head and added, 'And what is that hammering?'.

29

New York Harbour Feb 1922

Professor Jan Wouters knew he was the luckiest man alive. He was doing a job that he loved. It was a job that sometimes, just sometimes, allowed him to make trips such as this, to the new world. Ahhh, if only his forbears had had the good sense to keep a hold of this extraordinary place.

New Amsterdam was what they had called this place. Now it was New York. He glanced out towards the quay. Crowds of people were braving the rain to greet the arrival of the liner. He glanced up at the ominously dark cloud little realising that it was a portent. At that moment, he was feeling only optimism.

He had brokered a deal to have several great masterpieces from seventeenth century Dutch art returned on loan to the museum. One of them was a great self-portrait by Rembrandt. Their exhibition would now have most of the later portraits to add to a fine collection of the earlier ones. It would trace the life of one extraordinary mind who documented his life with unsparing honesty.

One day, the Americans would be unstoppable as they acquired more and more great European art. It seemed only he was aware of this threat. Of how so much that was displayed in the great houses of noblemen would slowly disappear as dissolute living, taxes and who knows what else, saw the great private collections getting sold off, to rapacious American billionaires.

It was inevitable. They could no more stop this process than order the tide to halt. Rather than fight what was going to happen anyway, the time had come to embrace the future.

These were his thoughts, as he stepped off the liner and walked down the gangplank and saw his friend from the museum waiting, quayside, to greet him. They shook hands and he climbed into the car. There were two men sitting in the front. Rather rough looking characters, in the view of Wouters, who had an element of the dilettante about him. Others would have described him as an inveterate snob.

'We'll have your luggage sent to the hotel,' they said.

The car set off and they headed towards the museum first. Wouters had been once before, just after the War ended. It was where the idea had been borne. As tempting as it was to join his friend to glimpse some of the treasures he was to take, they dropped his friend off and the cab set off to his hotel.

There was no sense of alarm as the journey seemed to take a little longer than he had envisaged. Doubts began to set in when he saw that they were outside the city. He tapped the man in the front passenger seat on the shoulder. His English was impeccable, arguably superior to that of his current travel companions, who had barely spoken throughout the journey.

'Excuse me, may I ask where you are taking me? This hotel seems further away than I thought?'

The man he addressed said nothing. Instead, he searched in his breast pocket for something and then pulled it out.

A gun.

Wouters realised at this point, they were not going to a hotel, there was going to be no loan to the Rijksmuseum. He was not feeling so lucky now. He felt like a damn fool. He was about to be a dupe for the greatest art theft in history.

30

'They're packing away the paintings for the loan to Amsterdam,' said Nolan, in answer to Bobbie's question.

Bobbie shut her eyes as she remembered earlier mentions of the loan. This probably was not a good idea because the state of her headache was not getting any better and opening her eyes once more took more of an effort than she wanted to let on. She put her hand up to her head in an involuntary gesture.

The two men immediately expressed concern for the young woman. Nolan glanced towards Devenish and wondered, briefly, if Bobbie viewed him as more than a friend. He certainly appeared to know Bobbie well and, equally, there was no question Bobbie appeared to like him.

'I remember Mr Robinson mentioned about loaning paintings to the Rijksmuseum,' said Bobbie, her voice tight now with the effort of hiding the pain she felt, physically as well as emotionally.

'Great timing,' said Devenish.

As he said this a strange thing happened. They all looked at one another in growing astonishment. Bobbie's mind was already in turmoil thanks to the anxiety she felt about her father and her headache. Yet, upon hearing Devenish say, "great timing", her mind suddenly fell into sharp focus. The murder of Coletti, finding the plans to steal William the Hippo and then its actual theft, her kidnapping. So many things that had occupied everyone's attention.

Could there have been a reason for this? A reason such as a desire to distract from something else. Looking at the two men, she could sense that similar thoughts were occurring to them. Outside the door of the storeroom the sound of the paintings being put into crates and loaded onto the waiting truck echoed around the large chamber.

It was Bobbie who gave voice to these thoughts.

'I can't believe I'm going to say this, but those paintings are almost priceless. There are Rembrandts and other Dutch masterpieces, going on loan. What if that is the real plan and not the theft of William, the Hippo? It would make more sense.'

The two men were silent. The silence, in Bobbie's view, suggested agreement. No other explanation of the peculiar events of the past twenty-fours remotely made sense, except this. The two men glanced at one another and then Devenish replied, 'It's too incredible. I mean, why take the risk with all these policemen around and, if I may say, my good self?'

'What risk were they taking?' asked Nolan. 'Think about it. They did not foresee Miss Flynn being in the museum today with Violet. Had they not been here, then William the Hippo would not have been found so quickly and they would not have had to kidnap Miss Flynn and then the inspector. Your presence, Miss Flynn, completely threw them. The original plan would have had everyone upstairs, investigating the theft, or the murder, while the real robbery took place under their noses.'

Devenish looked at Nolan, with something close to respect.

'Not bad for a cop, Nolan. Not bad. You have potential.'

'Thank you,' said Nolan, sardonically.

Bobbie couldn't decide if she was happy that Nolan was so well thought of or appalled by this. However, her growing feeling of nausea interrupted any further thought on that topic.

'We have to stop them,' she said, trying to control the urge to throw up.

'Who can we trust?' asked Devenish. 'I'm pretty sure Robinson is fine. We, clearly, can't trust Sampson, or any of the security men. Who is that patrolman?'

'Lewis,' replied Nolan. 'I'm not sure about him, I must admit. He's new. Came from Chicago. There's a cloud hanging over him.'

They walked over to the door of the storeroom and peeked outside. The floor of the storage area near the bay was clear now of all but one painting. They watched as the self-portrait of Rembrandt was wrapped in cotton cloth before being carefully loaded inside a narrow wooden crate. Then one of the security guards placed a lid on the crate and hammered it down.

Standing watching them do this were Sampson, Roscoe Meredith and a blonde-haired man that Bobbie did not recognise. She turned to Devenish and mouthed, 'Who is he?'

'That's Professor Wouters from the Rijksmuseum,' replied Devenish, before adding, in a murmur, 'Apparently.' He shook his head for a few moments and then spoke for all of them. 'Maybe we're being alarmist. For this to be a robbery, it would require an enormous conspiracy. You'd need Sampson, you'd need Meredith, possibly and some of the security guards like Coletti and Barnes, to be a party to the robbery. Dare I say, Edward Robinson too. I'm not sure I believe that myself.'

Bobbie was beginning to have grave doubts herself. She knew that she tended to see crime where, probably, none existed. It was part of the job of being a journalist on the crime desk, not just there in fact, she saw herself as part of a tradition, started by Nellie Bly, of investigative journalism. This required constant belief, optimism even, that there was a story lurking in the shadows, of any part of everyday life.

It was Nolan who emboldened them, however.

'I don't believe in coincidences. These paintings are not priceless. Someone, somewhere, will buy them. Or the museum will pay a mighty ransom. Either way, there is a lot of money to be made from stealing them.'

'But so many different people involved, Nolan?' asked Devenish, sceptically.

'You just need three,' replied Nolan. 'And you might be looking at them there.'

They looked out at the storage area as the last of the paintings was loaded onto the truck.

'Even if you think that Sampson is a bad lot, surely Robinson will know whether the man here, claiming to be Wouters, is genuine or fake, surely,' said Devenish, aghast at the rather cavalier treatment of a priceless set of paintings.

Robinson and Meredith stood alongside Sampson watching the truck slowly drive out of the storage area. It stopped just outside. It was raining. Light glinted off the puddles outside.

'What are we going to do?' asked Bobbie, fear and exasperation permeated her voice. This was not her area. As much as she wanted to be involved in the crime reporting and even the investigative side, being an eyewitness to a potential art theft had some downsides. Besides which, her head was thumping like a bass drum in tandem with her heart. And where was the ambulance?

'Have you a gun?' asked Nolan to Devenish.

The private investigator seemed a little embarrassed by the question. He hesitated before saying, 'In a manner of speaking.'

'What manner is that?' asked Nolan, impatiently, some of his previous irritation with the dandyish private investigator, returning.

'It's mainly as a last resort,' explained Devenish producing a small Derringer.

'You didn't want to ruin the lines of your suit,' said Bobbie a little more waspishly than she'd intended.

'It's tailor made, Italian silk lining, my darling,' replied Devenish, although, he did not seem to be put out by the sour comment from Bobbie.

His comment redeemed himself, a little, in Nolan's eyes as there wasn't a trace of fear in his voice. He was ready, for whatever had to be done. The two men exchanged glances. There was no fear in the private investigator's eyes. Instead, Nolan detected a cool, nerveless stare that seemed at odds with the flippant, rather arrogant, nature of the man. He was ready for the fight and, Nolan suspected, he would be a good man to have by his side.

'Stay here Red, it's time to play hero,' said Devenish, before adding, 'Again.'

Bobbie automatically rolled her eyes at her friend's uninhibited conceit, but she smiled too and nodded.

'On the count of three,' whispered Nolan. He held up a Colt.

'You go first,' said Devenish grimly, eyeing the large revolver and then holding up the, rather more diminutive, Deringer.

'Thanks,' replied Nolan sternly. 'One, two, three...'

31

Just as Nolan and Devenish burst through the door of the storeroom, into the main storage bay area, Lewis reappeared, along with Lieutenant Grimm, followed by Edward Robinson. The two policemen saw that both Nolan and Devenish had their guns drawn. Martinet he might be, but Grimm's hand immediately reached into his holster. In moments, Lewis was holding his weapon.

'Any reason for this?' murmured Grimm, to Nolan as they met up in the middle of the bay area. Nolan nodded to Grimm, but stayed silent, as they moved towards the museum employees. Nolan noticed, with satisfaction, that Devenish had moved to his right to cover Lewis in case there was any problem from that direction.

The arrival of the three policemen and Devenish had not gone unnoticed by Sampson, Meredith, Professor Wouters and the security guards who all turned around. The sight of the drawn guns was a surprise to them. And if it was surprise to them, it was a shock to Edward Robinson.

The head of the museum was acutely aware that the events of the day had frayed everyone's nerves, including his own and he was in the middle of his own battle to save the reputation of the museum with a senior curator of one of the great art institutions of the world.

'Is this really necessary?' asked Robinson, unable to hide the irritation in his voice.

Grimm glanced sideways at Nolan. It was a look that screamed – this-better-be-necessary.

'I'm sorry sir,' said Nolan. His voice was clear with no trace of fear. 'We just would like to check a few things.'

'Like what?' snapped Robinson. He was a man who normally exuded self-control, but there was a limit and it was perilously close to being reached.

Keeping his eyes on the museum men, Nolan said, 'The theft of the hippo was meant to be a distraction from what the robbers really intended.'

Robinson glanced from Nolan to the truck and then back to the detective.

'This is madness. The loan to the Rijksmuseum was planned months ago. You can't be seriously suggesting that Professor Wouters is going to steal these paintings.'

'I'm not accusing anyone,' replied Nolan. 'Yet. The truck will only be released when we are satisfied that everything is as it should be.'

Robinson was caught, between admiring the young man's determination to ensure the safety of the paintings and frustration at seeing, not only, a long-term initiative calamitously fail, but also how the reputation of the museum might be destroyed. He looked at the senior policeman and said, 'Lieutenant Grimm, is this necessary?'

Grimm was caught in the no man's land of indecision. If he made the wrong call here, it would be very damaging for a man who had set his sights on the highest office. Where was that man O'Riordan when he was needed? This should be his call.

In fact, the good captain was answering nature's call, just at that moment and would be along shortly. This was of no use to Grimm as he surveyed the scene, with all the enthusiasm of a man facing a firing squad, composed of his ex-wives.

Grimm looked at Nolan. He disliked Nolan. Always had. The reason he gave was that he sensed the young man did not like him. Yet Grimm was honest enough about himself to realise that he was also a little afraid of Nolan. The young man had gone to war and fought bravely. He was palpably a popular individual in the squad room. Worst of all, he was obviously very capable, with instincts that a sensible senior officer should respect.

Grimm's answer was to tread, as ever, the narrow line between supporting a colleague and, alternatively, giving him enough rope to hang himself.

'I'm sure there's nothing to be worried about, but perhaps, if we could just hold on, for one moment, while Detective Nolan satisfies himself that all is in order,' said Grimm. He emphasised the words "Detective Nolan", which did not go unnoticed by the young man, or Devenish, who grinned in perverse enjoyment at this.

'Can you ask the drivers to step out of the truck,' asked Nolan, to Sampson. The big Texan wasn't sure if he should have his hands up or hands down. This resulted in an odd compromise whereby they were by his side, gunfighter style.

'Are you sure about this son?' he drawled, lazily. There was a half-smile on his face.

'I'm sure,' said Nolan, who was only sure of one thing: he had no idea what he was doing. All he had to go on was a gut instinct that something was wrong and a trust that both Bobbie and Devenish shared his view, that the theft upstairs was misdirection.

Roscoe Meredith had been watching all of this with a growing sense of outrage. He turned to Nolan and said, in a voice of barely supressed rage, 'Who do you think you are?' he followed this up by spinning around to Robinson and saying, 'Edward are you really going to put up with this?'

Edward Robinson was certainly not going to put up with this. While he was not very pleased at Nolan's insistence on waiting, he was even less pleased by the intervention of Meredith, a man he had never really taken to, particularly as he had effectively questioned his authority, in permitting the policeman to make one last check.

Meredith almost froze, as he saw the ice-cold fury in Robinson's eyes. Just as he was about to stutter out an explanation of what he meant by this; he was halted by a wave of the Museum Director's hand.

'We'll talk about this later, Meredith,' said Robinson, with a voice tighter than a violin string. A trip to the headmaster's office beckoned for Meredith but, at least, it wasn't a public dressing down, he reasoned. 'Now, if Detective Nolan would like to proceed.'

Nolan nodded in gratitude to Robinson. Then he asked, 'What are the security arrangements in place?'

Devenish, who was behind Nolan answered this.

'I believe Mr Sampson and two cars will accompany the truck. One in front and one behind, Detective Nolan. They're parked outside. I'm not sure exactly who will be in the cars, aside from Wouters, perhaps Mr Sampson can confirm.'

The atmosphere in the storage area crackled with tension. All eyes turned to Sampson.

Sampson pointed to three security guards that Nolan hadn't seen before and said, 'I won't be in the cars, but these gentlemen will be. And Professor Wouters, as Mr Devenish mentioned.'

Nolan turned to Wouters and fixed his eyes on him. The professor was tall, slender and with fair hair. So far, he'd said little, beyond speaking excellent English in a guttural Dutch accent. He was in his forties and was perspiring in a manner that any sensible man would, if he was responsible for the shipment of a priceless collection of art.

What happened next was set off with three simple words, spoken in Dutch, by Nolan who had been taught them by a soldier he'd met in France nearly four years earlier. They were the only words of Dutch he knew.

'*Hoe is het?*' (How are you?)

An unmistakable look of panic exploded in the Dutch professor's eyes, principally because he spoke not a word of the language, having been brought up in San Antonio, where English and Spanish dominated. Nolan needed only an instant to register the fact that the man before him was no more Dutch than he was.

Unfortunately, this realisation was followed a split second later by the sound of two guns clicking and Meredith and Robinson saying in unison.

'Good Lord.'

And then the first shot rang out.

And then another.

And then, a few moments later, a third, followed swiftly by the fourth and final shot.

32

Bobbie watched, as Nolan and Devenish drew close to the men by the truck. At first, they did not seem to be aware that they were approaching and then, suddenly, the atmosphere changed, as it began to dawn on the museum men, that there were two men holding guns on them. Once again, Bobbie felt her heart racing.

Whatever her feelings towards Nolan and the word "mixed" barely covered the multitude of emotions this young man stirred within her, she did not want to see him or Devenish hurt. Yet, she was worried about the scenario they were facing. The arrival of the other policemen led by Grimm did not provide her with any more reassurance that the situation was anything other than dangerous.

Some, possibly all the men in the storage area, with the exception of Edward Robinson, were potentially conspiring to steal the paintings going on loan to Amsterdam. She stood looking at the scene unfold, listening to them speak and then a thought occurred to her.

She did not have to be a bystander to this after all.

Bobbie turned towards her father's coffin and ran towards it. Her father lay there and once more she fought to control the raging emotions that included anger, anguish and annoyance at the length of time it was taking for help to arrive.

'Sorry daddy,' she said before pulling aside his coat to find that Larry Barnes had been in such a rush to render her father unconscious, and then hide him, that he had forgotten to remove his weapon. She found what she was looking for, in a holster inside his coat.

Bobbie held up the Colt, a weapon that she had used, many times with her father, at the police shooting range. She had become quite a celebrity at the shooting range when she first started accompanying her father.

And later, a crack shot.

Bobbie rushed back to the door, just in time to see the exchange between Meredith and Robinson. She had only just met him that day, yet she had disliked him, almost immediately. He was arrogant and he was a bully. The feeling of antipathy intensified as she saw him treat Nolan dismissively. And then he tried this with Edward Robinson. Bobbie smiled grimly at this. She recognised a big mistake when she saw it. And this was a mistake.

However, Bobbie could not enjoy the sight of Meredith's humiliation for long because she was distracted by something else. The driver's door had opened and a man had stepped down from the cab. Initially he was a shadow but, slowly, he emerged into the light. He looked familiar.

He was in his thirties, with fair hair and a pale moustache. He seemed like the younger version of Edward Robinson, immortalised by Sargent in his portrait. While Bobbie racked her memory to put a name to the man's face, her eyes strayed down to his hand. He was carrying something. It glinted in the light.

There could be no doubt now she was witnessing a robbery. Worse, both Nolan and Devenish were exposed in the open along with the patrolman Lewis. The question was, who were the robbers? Not Robinson. Meredith? This seemed unlikely. To pull something like this off required a steely nerve. Unless Meredith was a great actor, he was not that kind of man.

Bobbie stared in horror as the man approached the storage area from the other side of the truck, hidden from Nolan and Devenish. What should she do? If she shouted a warning, they were no better off as both were surrounded by potential robbers. Bobbie hardly dared breathe as she watched the scene unfold.

And then, to her amazement she heard Nolan say something in a foreign language. Had he just spoken Dutch to the man from the Rijksmuseum? Bobbie's eyes swivelled over to Wouters. Nothing on the man's face suggested he had understood a single word Nolan had said.

Bobbie's eyes flicked back to the man hiding on the other side of the truck. He was raising his gun. There could be no question on what he was intending. Just at that moment Bobbie recognised the man.

In another part of the building, Captain Frank O'Riordan had just finished nature's call. He was a man famed for having a monumental bladder. He exited the bathroom without the slightest idea where everyone else had gone. Then he remembered that someone had mentioned looking for Inspector Flynn in the storage area of the museum basement. This, he reasoned, was as good a place as any to start.

Of course, he had not the slightest idea of where he should go. He returned to the scene of the robbery and found one of the museum ushers, an elderly gentleman by the name of Buckley Wainwright. The kindly old usher looked like a man who could be ordered around. His was rather overweight, which suggested he could do with a bit of exercise. He was as close to seventy as made no difference, egg-shaped, a small head atop a body that had spent too much of its life in repose.

'Hey you,' said O'Riordan. 'Take me to the basement, pronto.'

'Yes, sir,' said Buckley, a man who had devoted his life to helping people, even ones as rude as the captain. He'd watched O'Riordan in action and was less than impressed. Some of the younger men appeared to have more of an idea on police procedure than the captain. The man he was looking at seemed at home giving orders, even if he had no idea what he was trying to achieve.

They walked over to the door that had been used to abduct Bobbie. O'Riordan found himself in a stairwell that was a little less ornate than the opulent staircase which had taken him up to the scene of the crime. Or one of them anyway. It occurred to O'Riordan, at this point, just how many crimes the museum had witnessed over the previous twenty-four hours. It must have been something of a record. One murder, at least, two kidnappings potentially and one, maybe two, robberies. It was difficult to keep count of all that was happening, but one thing was clear in O'Riordan's mind. Catch one criminal and you had several crimes solved. And he would count each of them on his record.

They descended the stairs at a leisurely rate. Neither man was in a hurry. O'Riordan was more than happy to come in at the conclusion of the search, so why rush? He decided that his earlier manner with the old man had been somewhat peremptory. He decided to redress the balance by a little conversation.

'Been here long?' asked O'Riordan, to kick things off.

'Oh yes sir, I joined when the museum first opened,' said Wainwright.

This surprised O'Riordan so much he removed the cigar from the mouth in which it appeared to be permanently resident.

'Good grief! How long is that?' asked the captain, in astonishment, assuming that the museum had opened a hundred years earlier.

'Fifty-two years nearly,' answered the usher proudly. 'I joined when I was seventeen.'

O'Riordan didn't bother to calculate how old the usher was. This had just about exhausted O'Riordan's conversation, so they walked the rest of the way in a companionable silence.

They reached the corridor that led to the large double doors of the storage area. The ceilings were even higher here and it was noticeably colder in this part of the building. This led O'Riordan to complain that the museum was obviously saving money on their heating bills. Wainwright chuckled at this and decided that the captain wasn't nearly as bad as he'd first thought.

They reached the double doors. O'Riordan stopped to re-light his cigar. He turned to Wainwright and said, 'Is this it?'

'Yes, sir,' replied Wainwright. 'Will that be all?'

'I guess so,' said O'Riordan, replacing the cigar back in his mouth. He nodded a thanks to Wainwright and watched the old usher pootle off.

O'Riordan paused for a moment by the door, puffing contentedly on the cigar. With any luck they would have found the old man and his daughter, saving him a job. How difficult could it be anyway? The storage area would have been the first place he'd have looked. The clue was in the name, he thought to himself. He then decided it was time to make an appearance. Just as he was about to open the door, he heard something that had him reaching instinctively for his gun.

It sounded something like '*Hoe is het?*' to Bobbie's ears, but it produced an instant response from the man by the truck. And Bobbie knew him now. It was Thomas Hudson minus his beard. The man that was supposed to be going away on a dig to Egypt was, in fact, taking time off to do something else. Bobbie couldn't believe it.

And he was raising his gun a little bit uncertainly. He was not a man used to weapons, as far as Bobbie could tell, but she couldn't rely on this intuition. He was about ten yards away from her. She raised her gun and made the decision.

She cocked her trigger, a noise that seemed to echo around the storage room like a volley of muskets and fired at Hudson. The gun went flying out of his hand. Hudson was too shocked to scream in pain.

Nolan reacted immediately. He fell to the floor, just as Sampson pulled a gun from his holster, but before he could aim it at Nolan, Dick Devenish fired into the ground at Sampson's feet causing the Texan to dance a jig. He glanced at Devenish and dropped his weapon with a resigned smile.

By now Meredith and Robinson had both dived to the ground, deciding, not unreasonably, that this was a marginally safer place to be than standing in the way of the men with guns, while Hudson was moaning bitterly about his bloodied hand. Joining the men on the ground were some of the security guards who, although armed, were not in the mood for a firefight and, also, Lieutenant Grimm. The only people left standing in the storage area were Bobbie, by the storage room, Nolan, Devenish and Sampson.

Nolan turned towards Bobbie and nodded in appreciation of the fact that she had very probably saved his life. He stared at her for a moment. She was standing with two arms raised holding her weapon. Inspector Flynn had brought her up well. There was no sorrow in her eyes. At that moment, she resembled nothing less than a hunter. Nolan decided, there and then, that even if he married her, he would never cross her. He hoped that he would have the opportunity to put this to the test.

His next glance was for Devenish. He, too, had probably saved the young detective's life. Devenish still had his Deringer pointed at Sampson. Then he did something strange. He twisted around in the direction of Nolan.

And fired.

33

For the second time, he heard the click of a gun nearby. Nolan had no time to react. If this was it then he had to accept that Devenish had deceived them all brilliantly. He'd created an astonishing crime. He waited for the end. His eyes jerked shut at the sound of the gunshot.

He sensed the bullet whizz past his head. His eyes shot open, then widened in shock as he realised that he was still alive. Before he could inquire as to why Devenish had taken leave of his senses, he realised that the private detective's eyes were not focussed on him. Nolan turned around and saw a man dressed as a driver lying on the ground, clutching his shoulder and moaning.

It was Larry Barnes.

Bobbie had not seen Barnes. Initially she had only seen Devenish point his gun in the direction of Nolan. She'd not had time to react and then, to her astonishment, Devenish had seemed to fire at Nolan. And miss. It took a few moments for her to realise that the target was not Nolan, but the other driver, who had appeared on the blind side of the truck to her.

However, things had not finished yet. On the other side of Nolan, Sampson had dived to the ground when Devenish had shot at Barnes. He grabbed the weapon that he'd dropped. In a swift, practiced movement he had the weapon in his hand and was aiming to shoot Nolan. When another gunshot echoed around the chamber.

'Drop it, Sampson,' shouted Captain Frank O'Riordan. He strode forward like the sheriff of a small western town. The cigar never left his mouth as he glared first at Sampson, then at Nolan and finally at Devenish. His eyes squinted at the private detective, who was still holding his Deringer.

'Don't tempt me Devenish,' snarled O'Riordan. The private detective smiled and quickly lowered his weapon.

'I shan't Francis, old boy,' laughed Devenish.

O'Riordan surveyed the carnage before him. Two men were down, both drivers. He saw weapons near both, but neither seemed in a mood to take up the fight. His eyes fell on Robinson and Meredith who were both getting to their feet. Both seemed unharmed. Another, blond-haired, man stayed on the ground. O'Riordan didn't like the look of him.

'Now, will someone tell me what in the hell is going on here?' barked O'Riordan, through his clenched teeth.

Rather than answer him immediately, Nolan, Lewis and Devenish, as if reading each other's minds, ran over to Sampson, Hudson and Barnes to pick up their fallen weapons. The three men, two of whom were slightly wounded, plus Wouters, who was unarmed, were placed against the wall and handcuffed by all the available handcuffs, including the pair that, ironically for Barnes, he had used on Bobbie.

Before Nolan could properly thank Bobbie for saving his life, a siren heralded the arrival of the ambulance that would take Inspector Flynn away, as well as the two wounded men. They were to be transferred to a hospital first, to have their wounds attended to, before being remanded in custody.

Bobbie oversaw the removal of her father, while all the time conscious of Nolan's desire to say something to her. In truth, she was glad that she had the distraction of her father because she was afraid to face the detective. Nolan hovered around, not wanting to interrupt her concern for her father, with his own appeal for her attention. For her to see his gratitude. He was finally put out of his misery by Devenish, who tapped him on the shoulder.

'Not now,' he murmured. Then, grim-faced, Nolan nodded and watched as Devenish shouted over to Bobbie, 'Hey Red'.

Bobbie turned to Devenish. Her face was streaked with worried tears.

'Good shot,' said the private detective with a grin. 'I'd have taken his head off.'

Bobbie sketched a smile and replied, 'What makes you think I wasn't aiming there?'

Devenish laughed at this and shook his head, 'Somehow I doubt it.'

Then Bobbie glanced towards Nolan. Their eyes met briefly, before Bobbie looked away and followed the two ambulancemen towards their vehicle. She climbed into the back without looking back at Nolan. The doors closed and within a few moments the ambulance departed with Flynn and Bobbie. It was decided that Hudson and Barnes could go to the hospital in the back of a police car.

Nolan watched the ambulance go, joined by Devenish. He felt the private detective clap him on the back.

'Good work detective.'

'It was you, the captain and Bobbie who stopped them,' said Nolan, modestly.

'I wasn't referring to that,' said Devenish with a sly smile.

Nolan frowned and asked him what he meant. Devenish nodded towards the departing ambulance.

'Getting Red to fall for you like that.'

'It doesn't feel like it,' murmured Nolan gloomily, as much to himself as Devenish. Which brought a mirthless laugh from Devenish.

'I love that girl,' said Devenish. Oddly, Nolan did not feel jealous on hearing this. If anything, it felt oddly reassuring. Devenish seemed more like a comrade in arms, at that moment, than a love rival and Nolan wondered why.

Another man whose sense of satisfaction was oddly muted, at that moment, was Captain Francis O'Riordan. His delight at playing an instrumental role, in the capture of the robbers, was tempered, somewhat, by the news that it was Bobbie who had initially saved the day. However, he reasoned, that by the time he had written his report, his role would become the pivotal moment in the whole affair. And if Nolan had any sense, his report would in no way contradict this assertion.

The thought that Nolan would have to, through gritted teeth, acknowledge his captain's timely arrival, perked him up a bit and he sauntered over to the two young men watching the ambulance depart in a much better fettle.

'Good work boys,' he said expansively, knowing full well that such a compliment would demand some degree of reciprocation from the two men whose lives he had probably saved.

Devenish turned around and chuckled at O'Riordan. He regarded him for a moment, amusedly and shook his head in a form of contrition for ever having doubted the captain.

'Well, I have to say, Francis, old boy, you turned up trumps today. I think Nolan and I owe you one.'

'Nonsense, Devenish, you'd have done the same for me, I'm sure,' replied O'Riordan. He knew he was laying it on a bit thick but this, he hoped, would only increase the misery of the two men. Nolan turned to O'Riordan. The young man had a way of looking at you that O'Riordan found unsettling. Yet, for once, he did not find it so. Because this time there was something that he realised he had not seen before.

Respect.

Nolan nodded to O'Riordan. He said two words only, 'Thanks, sir.'

All sense of superiority for O'Riordan, evaporated at that moment. Rather than anger at this happening, something else rose within him which he found as unfathomable as much as he tried to deny it. He felt proud. Whatever plaudits were likely to come his way, following the successful conclusion to this case, he doubted that any would be as hard-earned as the one bestowed by the young detective, just at that moment.

34

One day later

Columbus Hospital 226 East 20th Street, New York: late February 1922

Bobbie sat by the bedside of her father, while Violet sat on the bed. Inspector Flynn was sitting up on the bed, with a bandaged head, accompanied by a face that was sour, even by his own standards. His head hurt damnably and he was in no mood to stay silent about this fact. Despite this, he was delighted to see his daughter and young Violet. He was even happier to hear that the case had been brought to a successful conclusion. Yet, he had not heard all the details of how this had happened.

In fact, worryingly, his daughter had spared quite a few of the details which meant only one thing in Flynn's mind: she had been heavily involved in the capture of Sampson, Hudson, Barnes and the fake Dutch curator from the Rijksmuseum. The question was who would fill in for him the details of what had happened. The answer was not long in coming.

Dick Devenish burst through the doors of the hospital room with all the wilful abandon of a child, clutching a water pistol. Without so much as a 'hello', he announced his arrival by saying, 'Do you know, I had the most extraordinary encounter, with one of your patrolmen, in the corridor.'

'Oh?' said Flynn.

'Yes, he said that you'd given express orders you were to have no visitors except police or family.'

'And yet, you are here,' pointed out Flynn, wearily.

'Naturally. I said that I was Red's fiancé. That did the trick pretty sharpish, I can tell you,' said Devenish brightly.

'You did what?' exclaimed Bobbie, Flynn and Violet in unison. Bobbie, it must be reported, was half laughing, but the others were outraged.

'I can't think of why your daughter won't marry me,' replied Devenish, impervious to the outrage from his prospective father-in-law.

'Do you want to hear my thoughts on the subject?' asked Flynn.

'I suspect they are irrelevant,' retorted Devenish, which was probably closer to the truth than Flynn would have liked to admit.

'To what do we owe the honour of your presence?' asked Flynn, anticipating the question Bobbie was about to ask, minus the sarcasm.

'Well, it occurred to me that, by the time Bobbie saw you off to the hospital, Flynn, old boy and then sent word to this young lady that all was well with the world, it would have left precious little time for her to be able to update you on the thrilling events of yesterday evening. You'd have enjoyed it Flynn, I'm sure. A daring robbery within a daring robbery, cracked by this young eyewitness extraordinaire,' said Devenish, indicating Violet, who beamed at this, 'and a certain good-looking private detective with a nose for solving the trickiest of crimes and a beautiful young reporter who saved the day with a crack shot...'

Devenish stopped at this as he saw Bobbie's face transform from smile to grimace in a heartbeat. It was then that the private detective remembered that Flynn had a somewhat hostile attitude towards Bobbie's penchant for investigating crime.

'Keep going Devenish,' snarled Flynn. 'Bobbie has been a little bit scant on some of the details of last night. I want to hear everything.'

Devenish smiled towards Bobbie, whose face might have been described as Sphinx-like, given their recent encounters with ancient Egypt.

'Your daughter is nothing if not modest,' observed Devenish.

'Oh, that it were contagious,' scowled Flynn. 'Come on. Out with it, Dick.'

Devenish felt he was on sticky ground if Bobbie's face was anything to go by and looked for an escape route. He said, gaily, 'I wouldn't want to steal Red's thunder. That's quite a gal you have there, Flynn. She'll make some unlucky man, a hellishly difficult wife someday.'

'Thanks, Dick,' said Bobbie, unable to supress the smile that broke out on her face.

'You're welcome,' replied Devenish. 'Well, as you ask, Flynn old boy, you may as well get the scoop from me as from anyone else.'

Violet clapped her hands at this, while Bobbie's face took on a more disapproving mien once more. Devenish grabbed a chair and sat himself down.

'Picture the scene,' said Devenish, his arm slowly panning across an imaginary stage. 'You're napping away in your sarcophagus, Flynn. Incidentally, a few more bandages across your head and you would look like a mummy. Anyway, before you interrupt me once more, I digress. You are in your crypt, so to speak. Bobbie is with you, but by the door of the storeroom. Nolan and me, with no thought for our own safety, are approaching the truck full of priceless Dutch art. Neither of us knows friend or foe. We are armed only with our wits and a...'

'Deringer,' interrupted Bobbie, a wicked smile on her face.

'A Deringer?' laughed Flynn, amused by his daughter's mockery of Devenish.

'It did the job as you will hear,' said Devenish, just a hint of defensiveness in his tone. 'Anyway, we are surrounded by men that we, with Red's help, have reason to believe are committing a daring robbery. We know this because, and I will draw a modest veil here over my own contribution, we had recovered William the Hippo and had concluded this was merely a diversion for the real robbery. So, we have Nolan and me standing out in the open. We are facing Professor Wouters from Amsterdam who is near the truck, a couple of security guards, our Texan friend Sampson, more of him later, and that useless martinet, Meredith.'

'I'm guessing Meredith was not one of the gang,' said Flynn drily.

'Your powers of deduction do you credit, sir,' replied Devenish. 'Utter wet fish in my book. He looks the sort of man that would have snitched on his friends stealing candy from a store.'

'Did you ever do that?' asked Bobbie mischievously.

'Steal or snitch?' laughed Devenish. 'All I'll say is that I'm a poacher turned gamekeeper now. Anyway, enough of my criminal past. Onto Miss Annie Oakley, here and her role in foiling the gang. Maybe you should own up to your contribution, Red.'

Bobbie shook her head. In truth, she was assailed by a sudden onset of modesty, added to a little bit of fear that her father would be angry at her, once more, putting herself in harm's way. Besides which, she was rather enjoying Devenish telling the story. He was nothing if not entertaining.

'No?' said Devenish. 'Well, back to the scene. Nolan and I, exposed in the middle, little realising that we were about to be attacked from the flank. Bobbie, quick thinking as ever, grabbed the gun from a police inspector, who was asleep on duty...'

'Dick!' exclaimed Bobbie, in a tone of horror, that was somewhat undermined by the fact she was laughing.

'Napping away,' continued Devenish, ignoring the scowl on Flynn's face that was desperately hiding his smile. 'She had spotted, you'll never believe this, Thomas Hudson, newly shaved, approaching from our blindside.'

'Hudson?' interjected Flynn.

'Yes, Hudson,' said Bobbie. 'He'd made it known that he was going on an archaeological dig, which was true. This was his cover for masterminding the robbery.'

'He was the mastermind?'

'Him and Sampson. He was the one that suggested they hire Sampson.'

'But how did he know Sampson would turn bad. I thought his spell in prison was because he had attacked a racist police captain.'

'No,' said Devenish, a little sheepishly. 'It was the other way around. Sampson was the racist. He attacked his police captain who wanted to jail him, for near killing someone in a bar fight. Let's just say, Sampson had a lot of people who sympathised with his view on the Civil War and they faked his records so that it would appear he was a good guy. I'm afraid I was taken in by this too.'

'How did Hudson know?' asked Bobbie.

'Despite Hudson's rather refined accent, he originally comes from Texas. He'd read about the story when it first happened and then, later, saw that Sampson had been released. He did some checking and he heard that Sampson was a bad lot, in every respect. He put the proposition to Sampson who, shall we say, had effectively gone to a criminal university in his time in prison. Together they developed the plan.'

'Why was Nick Coletti killed?' asked Bobbie. This had always struck her as strange, as it had effectively created an air of suspicion around the museum.

'Sampson came clean on this – he's keen to avoid the chair. Barnes killed Coletti, he says. Apparently, they got into an argument. Coletti was threatening to blow the whole deal, so Barnes killed him. When Sampson and Hudson found out, they were incandescent. It was Hudson who decided to make a virtue of necessity. They planted the details of a potential theft of William the Hippo as potential misdirection for the real crime because they knew the police would be called to investigate Coletti's disappearance. They weren't counting on you, Red, being at the museum with your dad. That was when things started to spiral out of control. Kidnapping you, then you, Flynn, was not in the plan. Of all the days for you to visit the museum. Your timing was exquisite.'

'So, was this Professor Wouters a fake?' asked Flynn.

Devenish shook his head and said, 'Yes and no. The real Wouters is alive and well. They found him in a warehouse somewhere in Yonkers. Hudson met him a year ago and I think this is when the plan was formed because Wouters had never met any of the museum's art department. Hudson kept the contact going and he was the one who planted the seed to both Wouters and then Edward Robinson, about the possibility of a loan. Edward thought it a capital idea. Both he and Hudson persuaded the board at the museum to sanction the loan. This set off the chain of events that led to you ending up in hospital, looking like an Egyptian mummy, Flynn, old boy.'

'Very funny,' said Flynn, who was still feeling the effects of the crack on the head. Bobbie put a consoling arm around her father's shoulders. She sensed he was in a pain, but she also knew that Flynn would not admit to what extent he was feeling this, as he was grumpy at the best of times, as well as the worst.

'It looks like you have another scoop on your hands, Red,' said Devenish.

There was a knock on the door at this point. The door opened to reveal a rather mixed group of men, who entered one by one.

The first man through, carrying flowers and a box of chocolates, was Edward Robinson. He was followed, rather surprisingly, by Captain O'Riordan. For once he was missing the cigar clamped in his mouth. It did little to improve his appearance and only made his mood seem even darker. The most surprising visitor came last. He was in his mid-fifties and permanently wore an expression of satisfaction for a job well done. Flynn quite liked him. This was Richard Enright, the Police Commissioner for the New York Police Department. He took one look at his police inspector and chuckled, 'Don't get up Flynn.'

This brought a smile to Bobbie and Devenish's face. Bobbie glanced behind Enright, to see if anyone else was coming. Much to her disappointment, there was no one else. Just at that moment, she caught the eye of Devenish. He smiled knowingly at her, which made the colour of her face almost match that of her hair.

Enright was also carrying chocolates, which he handed to Flynn.

'I'd have brought you something more worthwhile, but alas that's not possible,' said Enright. He had sworn to uphold the law on Prohibition but recognised it had brought enormous problems with it for the police department. He did, however, reach into his pocket and pull out a cigar which he handed to Flynn.

'I seem to be going through these a lot faster than I should be,' murmured Enright, little suspecting they were being filched by Sergeant Harrigan.

'You didn't have to, sir,' said Flynn, looking guiltily at the cigar.

'I think I did,' said Enright and Flynn immediately detected something in the tone of his boss. He wondered what was to follow.

'What have we missed?' asked Robinson. 'Have Bobbie and Dick filled you in on the extraordinary events of yesterday evening, Flynn?'

'They have,' said Flynn unhappily.

'Bobbie is quite the hero,' said Robinson. 'We all owe her a great debt.'

'Nonsense,' said Devenish. 'She has all she needs.'

'You mean, her father's recovery?' asked Robinson.

'No,' said Devenish. 'She has a story. A front page story.'

Silence fell on the room. Robinson glanced towards Enright and shifted awkwardly in his stance. Enright coloured a little and cleared his throat. Before he could say anything, Bobbie filled the void.

'I don't have a story, do I?' said Bobbie, reading the faces of the two men that had entered.

'I'm sorry Bobbie,' said Robinson and he clearly meant it. His face was downcast and his voice was barely a whisper.

'What on earth?' said Devenish, a little loudly.

'No Dick, I understand,' said Bobbie. 'We can't talk about what happened. If I did, the museum would become a laughing stock around the world. No one would trust them with future loans. The number of bequests would decline. The ripple effects of this would be disastrous for the museum and for the city.'

Robinson looked at Bobbie fondly and said, 'I have always thought you a remarkable young woman, Bobbie and never more so than now. I'm so sorry. You do understand.'

Bobbie nodded and smiled, 'Yes. Yes, I do. There's no other way.'

Richard Enright was a rather relieved man, as it had been he who would have had to break the news to Bobbie. He said, 'You know if there's any way, we can make this up to you, please let me know.'

Bobbie smiled and shook her head, 'I'm not sure I can think of anything Commissioner Enright.'

'I can,' said a voice.

All eyes turned to Violet, who had been watching all the unfolding story, quietly. There were tears in her eyes, which shocked Bobbie, because Violet was not one to cry easily.

'I can think of something you can do, if it's in your power, Commissioner,' said the young girl.

35

Sing Sing Prison, Ossining, New York: late Feb 1922

Thirty miles north of New York is an institution with a musical name, but for the people housed there, life was anything but entertaining. Sing Sing prison was first opened one hundred years previously, taking its name from the Native American tribe, the Sintsink, who had lived there previously. It was, euphemistically, described as a Correctional Facility, which was operated by the New York State Department of Corrections and Community Supervision. Given that many of the inmates, who went there, ended up in the electric chair, it must be questioned just how committed to the idea of correction this august body was.

Renat Murdrych also known as Renat the Russian to a certain class of folk in New York, was now an inmate of Sing Sing, awaiting a trial that would, almost certainly, confirm that his residence would be extended for many years. Renat, if you remember, was a Russian immigrant, who had already escaped one penitentiary which was arguably even less welcoming than this one, in Siberia. He was now lodging in the prison as a consequence of kidnapping Violet Belmont. His capture had been somewhat self-inflicted, as he had all but given himself up in order to rescue the child, in an adventure described in another chronicle.

He viewed his impending trial with a certain fatalistic equanimity. Life had dealt him a bad hand, he'd lost his wife soon after the Russian revolution, he'd chosen the losing side in the subsequent civil war and he'd ended up in Siberia, before escaping the salt mines for a new life in America.

Renat was closer to seven feet tall than six and he had the build and strength, of a grizzly bear. Such impressive physical credentials made him an ideal employee for a certain sector of the American economy, that was expanding at an alarming rate following the passing of the Volstead Act prohibiting the sale of alcohol: crime.

Renat had spent the previous few years employed gainfully by several criminal gangs in New York. His limited command of English, combined with a morally neutral view towards violence, made him a natural enforcer. He enjoyed the job, in a manner of speaking, as his appearance often rendered violence unnecessary.

In Sing Sing, however, he was in the midst of many men who were, not so much morally neutral, as utterly devoid of any scruples. When many such men are placed together in the small confines of a building, notably lacking in any facilities that might educate or entertain the residents, then the inmates are likely to seek alternative forms of amusement.

A book was running on who would be the first, to not only engage the big Russian physically, but defeat him one on one. Renat was vaguely aware of this so he kept himself to himself. For the most part, the other inmates were happy to leave him, while a champion was found.

Those running the prison, the warden and the guards, were also aware that such a bet was in the air, although the former hoped that the latter would ensure it was never carried through. Such a desire was misplaced, as the guards themselves were running the book.

Warden Lewis E. Lawes stood at his office window, which overlooked the prison yard. Below him were the very worst of American society. He did not view them this way, although he was under no illusions about what type of men were incarcerated at the institution. He was barely eighteen months into his tenure. There was so much he wanted to achieve. Given the opportunity, he knew he could reform some of these men. There were some who were beyond redemption. His eyes fell upon the big Russian who had arrived only a couple of days earlier.

'Tell me, Sanders,' he said, to a guard who had come to see him with a report on the previous day's activities and misdemeanours. 'What do you reckon on that new guy? The Russian, I mean?'

Samuel Sanders had ten bucks on Renat not lasting the week. It was an outside bet, but the odds had been generous, because few had believed that anyone would be foolish enough to take on Renat. That said, common sense was not necessarily in much supply given the nature of the residents. It took Sanders a moment to work out if the warden was asking to throw his hat into the ring, with regard to the book on the Russian, before realising this was unlikely.

'Could be a target Mr Lawes,' said Sanders, choosing to take the opportunity to prime the warden on the potential for violence against the Russian.

'Really?' asked Lawes.

'Well, sir, abducting a child. No one takes kindly to that, sir.'

'I gather he saved her life too,' pointed out Lawes. 'The court may go easier on him.' Lawes was fully aware of the potential for violence against the Russian. He also had his suspicions about the man he was speaking to and the existence of illicit betting in the facility.

'That may not be common knowledge, sir,' said Sanders, shifting a little uncomfortably. He walked over to the window to join the warden. It was impossible to miss Renat. Even in a yard full of men, many quite large, Renat stood out, like a beacon of potential violence.

'Was it a good idea, then, for him to be allowed out into the yard. He is, after all, only on remand. Quite why they sent him here is beyond me.'

It was beyond Sanders too, but there was no question on one issue. Renat was a guilt-edged target and there was money to be made from his presence in the jail.

'Don't ask me,' laughed Sanders uneasily. At this point he realised that he should probably suggest that the big Russian leave the prison yard. This was not ideal as he knew that at least one inmate had backed himself to take out the Russian. His name was Clarence Kilmer. He was well-named, although his prison sentence came nowhere close to reflecting the true nature of his crimes. He was doing three years for assault.

From where Sanders was standing, he could see that a circle was slowly beginning to form. This was for two reasons.

202

It would provide the nearest with a great view of the fight while, at the same time, denying the guards a view of who was involved, although they could probably guess.

Sanders was keen to move the warden away from the window, as it would soon be apparent to him what was about to happen. Before he could suggest they go through the previous day's activities, Lawes exclaimed, 'I don't like the look of this.'

Nor did Renat.

He was by no means an intellectual, but he knew how to read a room, or in this case, a yard. All around him, he saw men looking at him, as if he were some exotic animal in a zoo. He acknowledged his size and his accent probably made him so.

There was no question in his mind, a circle was slowly forming. Without trying to reveal his hand he tried to keep a look out for where the attack would come from. He had already marked a couple of men as potential opponents due to their size. Unfortunately, they were also aware of this and were standing at opposite ends of the narrowing circle.

It was time to take matters into his own hands. Renat strode forward into the middle of the, still wide, circle. He bent his knees slightly and scanned around him for the anticipated attack.

The circle narrowed.

Renat felt his heartbeat rise. He was not afraid, but his senses were tingling and his muscles tensed, for what was to come.

The circle continued to narrow. It felt like a tourniquet. He knew the attack would happen soon.

He was right.

Kilmer timed his move for the moment that Renat's head turned towards the other likely candidate. He sprang forward, a razor inserted into a small wooden stick. The faces of the men in front of Renat provided the warning he needed because he had heard nothing. Renat sprang forward himself, narrowly missing the deadly blade.

He was now facing Kilmer. The man in front of him was a couple of inches shorter than he was, leaner and probably very fast. Of the two men he had suspected would attack him, this was the one he would have preferred to avoid.

Confidence poured from the eyes of his assailant. He fancied his chances against the big, lumbering Russian. The blade was just a hedge, though. No point in taking unnecessary risks. And he had to be quick. The guards would be in the yard in a matter of seconds. His blade sliced through the air once more.

Success!

He nicked Renat's bicep. The pain was almost blinding to Renat and he knew the next attack might be the last. Blood seeped from his wound. The sting was unbearable, but slowly eased as he braced himself for the next assault.

The former boxer, Kilmer, feinted to Renat's left and then lashed towards the Russian's body. It was, after all, quite a big target. To his surprise and perhaps Renat's, the blade missed by an inch, sending Kilmer slightly off balance. This left his ribcage open to an attack from Renat.

The kidney punch that sent Kilmer and the blade clattering to the ground was felt by everyone in the prison yard that witnessed it. Kilmer collapsed in agony, curling up into a foetal position, such was his distress.

Renat stepped forward and picked up the blade. He looked at it, the blood dripped down from it.

His blood.

He felt a wave of anger assail him. Around him he sensed the intake of breath and then he heard the siren wailing, the shouts of the guards and the moaning of the man who had just tried to kill him.

It would be so easy.

But no. Not today.

Renat hurled the blade so high and so far, that it flew over the wall of the prison yard and was probably heading towards Canada such was the violence of the throw.

By the time the guards had made their way through to the scene of the fight, Renat had melted into the crowd leaving only Kilmer lying on the ground, rueing his decision to pick on the big Russian.

Up in the office, the two men saw the guards beat their way through, only to find one man lying prone on the ground.

'Thank goodness they're through. Who is that?' asked Lawes, squinting to see who had lost and if they were alive or dead.

The guards helped, a rather reluctant, Kilmer to his feet. He was almost white with pain and quickly bent double once more. This was met with precious little sympathy from a couple of the guards, who'd backed Renat. They half dragged him off the yard, stopping once for the distressed prisoner to be ill.

Meanwhile, up in the warden's office, Sanders groaned inwardly. Ten bucks had just taken a beating. He was not happy. He would have to find a way of getting his own back on the man who had cost him so dearly.

And he would make him pay.

The End

Research Notes

This is a work of fiction. However, it references real-life individuals. Gore Vidal, in his introduction to Lincoln, writes that placing history in fiction or fiction in history has been unfashionable since Tolstoy and that the result can be accused of being neither. He defends the practice, pointing out that writers from Aeschylus to Shakespeare to Tolstoy have done so with, not inconsiderable, success and merit.

I have mentioned a number of key real-life individuals and events in this novel. My intention, in the following section, is to explain a little more about their connection to this period and this story.

Metropolitan Museum of Art

'The Met' is the largest museum in the Americas and the 4th largest in the world. The museum was founded in 1870 with a mission to bring art and art education to the American people. The museum's permanent collection consists of works of art ranging from ancient Egypt, through classical antiquity, to the modern world. It includes paintings and sculptures from many European old masters as well as an extensive collection of American, modern and contemporary art. The collection grew rapidly in the early twentieth century, when the museum was under the stewardship of Edward Robinson, who helped fuel the number of artworks bequeathed, thanks to the relationship with Joseph Duveen and the growth of American wealthy benefactors.

Edward Robinson (1858 – 1931)

Robinson was a Harvard graduate, who spent his early years as an archaeologist. Robinson became curator of classical antiquities at the Boston Museum of Fine Arts in 1885 a post he held until 1902 when he became the director. From 1906 he became Assistant Director of the Metropolitan Museum in New York. He took over as head of the museum in 1920. The portrait by Sargent was painted in 1903.

Joseph Duveen (1869 – 1939)

Along with his brother, Henry, the Duveens cornered the market in sales to the burgeoning class of American millionaires and multi-millionaires. Their sales pitch was simple, they offered a curated service to the very best of European art and the prospect of creating a legacy by bequeathing what they purchased to the growing number of American art institutions and securing a legacy of altruism and patriotism. Their client list, in America, was a who's who of tycoons: Clients included: Henry Frick, William Randolph Hearst, Benjamin Altman, Andrew Mellon, John D Rockefeller Sr, JP Morgan.

Rembrandt (1606 – 1669)

Quite simply, one of the greatest painters ever to have lived. A painter during the Golden Age of Dutch art, his works depict a wide range of styles from portraits and, particularly, his self-portraits, to landscapes, genre scenes, allegorical and historical scenes, biblical and mythological themes. The painting, referred to in the book, is a self-portrait completed in

1660 when he was fifty-four and facing financial ruin from his creditors. The following is its journey to the Metropolitan Museum:
- Unknown date: Duc de Valentinois, Paris between 15 July 1802 and 17 July 1802: anonymous sale at Lebrun, Paris (auction house)
- 1825: William Waldergrave (1753-1825)
- 1826: purchased by Alexander Baring, 1st Baron Ashburton
- 1908: Arthur J. Sulley & Co. (art dealers), London
- 1909/1910: obtained by Charles Sedelmeyer (art dealer), Paris
- 1909/1910: purchased by Benjamin Altman (1840-1913), New York
- 1913: bequeathed to Metropolitan Museum of Art, New York, by Benjamin Altman, New York

William the Hippo

William is the nickname given to this small, Egyptian Middle Kingdom statuette of a hippopotamus. The figurine was made in the 12th Dynasty ($c.$1961-1878 BC) and was placed with another in a tomb. Measuring just 11.2cm in height and 20cm in length, it was bright blue, with a body decorated with vegetal motifs symbolising regeneration – open and closed lotus flowers, buds and leaves. The statuette was excavated by Sayyid Pasha Khashaba in May 1910. It is one of a pair, found in the burial chamber of the nomarch, Senbi II, at Meir. The figure was acquired by the Metropolitan Museum of Art, New York, in 1917 and it is still on display. It was first dubbed 'William' by Captain H M Raleigh, who wrote in the satirical British magazine *Punch* in March 1931 – this is nine years later than when the story is set so I will admit to a little artistic license here!

Richard Enright (1871 - 1953)

Richard Enright was New York Police Commissioner between 1918 - 1925. This was a tumultuous time in the history of the country, not just the NYPD. He led a police force that was expanding at the same time as the Prohibition law was passed (1920) which gave rise to bootlegging and the growth of the Mafia in the US.

Enright was the first Police Commissioner to come up from the rank and file. This grounding gave him an insight into the life of everyday police work and meant that he was, despite his undoubted political nous, a man who earned the respect of the men under him. He brought in a number of reforms which improved working conditions for police officers, while in office.

He resigned in 1925 following criticism of the corruption that was endemic in the NYPD at this time. After trying, and failing, to press charges against thirteen police inspectors, he resigned one day before his term of office was due to expire.

Enright was a highly eloquent man, noted for his interest in the arts and history.

Sing Sing Prison, New York State (1825 - present day)

Sing Sing prison, originally called Ossining Correctional Facility has been a high-security prison since 1825. Located just north of New York, it was also a location of an execution chamber up until capital punishment was outlawed in New York state in 1970.

(Warden) Lewis E. Lawes (1883 - 1947)

Lewis E Lawes spent 21 years at Sing Sing, becoming warden in 1920, a post he held until his retirement in 1941. During his tenure, he instituted many reforms and was an opponent of capital punishment. He featured on the cover of

Time magazine in 1929 and one of his books, Twenty Thousand Years in Sing Sing, was made into a film in 1932 starring a young Spencer Tracy.

About the Author

Jack Murray was born in Northern Ireland but has spent over half his life living just outside London, except for some periods spent in Australia, Monte Carlo, and the US.

An artist, as well as a writer, Jack's work features in collections around the world and he has exhibited in Britain, Ireland, and Monte Carlo.

A spin off series from the Kit Aston novels was published in 2020 featuring Aunt Agatha as a young woman solving mysterious murders.

Another spin off series features Inspector Jellicoe. It is set in the late 1950's/early 1960's.

Jack finished work on a World War II trilogy in 2022. The three books look at the war from both the British and the German side. They have been published through Lume Books and are available on Amazon.

Acknowledgements

It is not possible to write a book on your own. There are contributions from so many people either directly or indirectly over many years. Listing them all would be an impossible task.

Special mention therefore should be made to my wife and family who have been patient and put up with my occasional grumpiness when working on this project.

My brother, Edward, has helped in proofing and made supportive comments that helped me tremendously. Thank you, too, Dave Robertson, Debra Cox, David Sinclair, Nathalie Pettus and Anna Wietrzychowska who have been a wonderful help in reducing the number of irritating errors that have affected my earlier novels. A word of thanks to Charles Gray and Brian Rice who have provided legal and accounting support.

My late father and mother both loved books. They encouraged a love of reading in me. In particular, they liked detective books, so I must tip my hat to the two greatest writers of this genre, Sir Arthur and Dame Agatha.

Following writing, comes the business of marketing. My thanks to Mark Hodgson and Sophia Kyriacou for their advice on this important area. Additionally, a shout out to the wonderful folk on 20Booksto50k.

Finally, my thanks to the teachers who taught and nurtured a love of writing.

Printed in Great Britain
by Amazon